V.S. Naipaul

VINTAGE **NAIPAUL**

V. S. Naipaul was born, of Indian ancestry, in Trinidad in 1932. He went to England in 1950. He spent four years at University College, Oxford, and began to write, in London, in 1954. He has pursued no other profession.

His works of fiction are *The Mystic Masseur* (1957; John Llewellyn Rhys Memorial Prize), *The Suffrage of Elvira* (1958), *Miguel Street* (1959; Somerset Maugham Award), *A House for Mr. Biswas* (1961), *Mr. Stone and the Knights Companion* (1963; Hawthornden Prize), *The Mimic Men* (1967; W. H. Smith Award), and *A Flag on the Island* (1967), a collection of short stories. In 1971 he was awarded the Booker Prize for *In a Free State*; since then he has published five novels: *Guerrillas* (1975), *A Bend in the River* (1979), *The Enigma of Arrival* (1987), *A Way in the World* (1994), and *Half a Life* (2001).

In 1960 he began to travel. *The Middle Passage* (1962) records his impressions of colonial society in the West Indies and South America. *An Area of Darkness* (1964), *India: A Wounded Civilization* (1977), and *India: A Million Mutinies Now* (1990) form his acclaimed "Indian Trilogy." *The Loss of El Dorado,* a masterly study of New World history, was published in 1969, and a selection of his longer essays, *The Overcrowded Barracoon,* appeared in 1972. *The Return of Eva Perón* (with *The Killings in Trinidad*) (1980) derives from experiences of travel in Argentina, Trinidad, and the Congo. *Finding the Center* (1984) is distinguished by the author's narrative on his emergence as a writer, "Prologue to an Autobiography." *A Turn in the South* (1989) describes his journey through the American South.

Among the Believers: An Islamic Journey (1981), a large-scale work, is the result of seven months' travel in 1979 and 1980 in Iran, Pakistan, Malaysia, and Indonesia. Its important sequel, *Beyond Belief* (1998), is on the theme of Islamic conversion in these countries.

Between Father and Son, the early correspondence between the author and his family, appeared in 1999.

In 1990, V. S. Naipaul received a knighthood for services to literature; in 1993, he was the first recipient of the David Cohen British Literature Prize in recognition of a "lifetime's achievement of a living British writer." He was awarded the Nobel Prize in Literature in 2001.

VINTAGE NAIPAUL

V. S. Naipaul

VINTAGE BOOKS

A Division of Random House, Inc.

New York

Library of Congress Cataloging-in-Publication Data

Naipaul, V. S. (Vidiadhar Surajprasad), 1932–
Vintage Naipaul / V. S. Naipaul.
1st Vintage Books ed.
p. cm.
1-4000-3400-0
Prologue from A house for Mr. Biswas—Chapter one from A house for
Mr. Biswas—Jasmine—Synthesis and mimicry—A new king for Congo—
Jack's garden—The Bomoh's son—From Half a life.
Naipaul, V. S. (Vidiadhar Surajprasad), 1932–
1. Travel.
2. Immigrants—England—Fiction.
3. Trinidad and Tobago—Fiction.
4. Trinidad and Tobago.
5. England—Fiction.
PR9272.9.N32 A6 2004
823'.914 22
2003057567

CONTENTS

VINTAGE **NAIPAUL**

Ten weeks before he died, Mr. Mohun Biswas, a journalist of Sikkim Street, St. James, Port of Spain, was sacked. He had been ill for some time. In less than a year he had spent more than nine weeks at the Colonial Hospital and convalesced at home for even longer. When the doctor advised him to take a complete rest the *Trinidad Sentinel* had no choice. It gave Mr. Biswas three months' notice and continued, up to the time of his death, to supply him every morning with a free copy of the paper.

Mr. Biswas was forty-six, and had four children. He had no money. His wife Shama had no money. On the house in Sikkim Street Mr. Biswas owed, and had been owing for four years, three thousand dollars. The interest on this, at 8 percent, came to twenty dollars a month; the ground rent was ten dollars. Two children were at school.

The two older children, on whom Mr. Biswas might have depended, were both abroad on scholarships.

It gave Mr. Biswas some satisfaction that in the circumstances Shama did not run straight off to her mother to beg for help. Ten years before that would have been her first thought. Now she tried to comfort Mr. Biswas, and devised plans on her own.

"Potatoes," she said. "We can start selling potatoes. The price around here is eight cents a pound. If we buy at five and sell at seven—"

"Trust the Tulsi bad blood," Mr. Biswas said. "I know that the pack of you Tulsis are financial geniuses. But have a good look around and count the number of people selling potatoes. Better to sell the old car."

"No. Not the car. Don't worry. We'll manage."

"Yes," Mr. Biswas said irritably. "We'll manage."

No more was heard of the potatoes, and Mr. Biswas never threatened again to sell the car. He didn't now care to do anything against his wife's wishes. He had grown to accept her judgment and to respect her optimism. He trusted her. Since they had moved to the house Shama had learned a new loyalty, to him and to their children; away from her mother and sisters, she was able to express this without shame, and to Mr. Biswas this was a triumph almost as big as the acquiring of his own house.

He thought of the house as his own, though for years it had been irretrievably mortgaged. And during these months of illness and despair he was struck again and again by the wonder of being in his own house, the audacity of it: to walk in through his own front gate, to bar entry to whoever he wished, to close his doors and windows every night, to hear no noises except those of his family, to wander freely from room to room and about his yard, instead of being condemned, as before, to retire the moment he got home to the crowded room in one or the other of Mrs. Tulsi's houses, crowded with Shama's sisters, their husbands, their children. As a boy he had moved from one house of strangers to another; and since his marriage he felt he had lived nowhere but in the houses of the Tulsis, at Hanuman House in Arwacas, in the decaying wooden house at Shorthills, in the clumsy concrete house in Port of Spain. And now at the end he found himself in his own house, on his own half-lot of land, his own portion of the earth. That he should have been responsible for this seemed to him, in these last months, stupendous.

The house could be seen from two or three streets away and was known all over St. James. It was like a huge and squat sentry-box: tall, square, two-storied, with a pyramidal roof of corrugated iron. It had been designed and built by a solicitor's clerk who built houses in his spare time. The solicitor's clerk had many contacts. He bought

land which the City Council had announced was not for
sale; he persuaded estate owners to split whole lots into
half-lots; he bought lots of barely reclaimed swampland
near Mucurapo and got permission to build on them. On
whole lots or three-quarter-lots he built one-story houses,
twenty feet by twenty-six, which could pass unnoticed;
on half-lots he built two-story houses, twenty feet by
thirteen, which were distinctive. All his houses were assem-
bled mainly from frames from the dismantled American
Army camps at Docksite, Pompeii Savannah and Fort
Read. The frames did not always match, but they enabled
the solicitor's clerk to pursue his hobby with little professional help.

On the ground floor of Mr. Biswas's two-story house
the solicitor's clerk had put a tiny kitchen in one corner;
the remaining L-shaped space, unbroken, served as drawing room and dining room. Between the kitchen and the
dining room there was a doorway but no door. Upstairs,
just above the kitchen, the clerk had constructed a concrete room which contained a toilet bowl, a wash-basin
and a shower; because of the shower this room was per-
petually wet. The remaining L-shaped space was broken
up into a bedroom, a verandah, a bedroom. Because the
house faced west and had no protection from the sun, in
the afternoon only two rooms were comfortably habit-
able: the kitchen downstairs and the wet bathroom-and-
lavatory upstairs.

In his original design the solicitor's clerk seemed to have forgotten the need for a staircase to link both floors, and what he had provided had the appearance of an afterthought. Doorways had been punched in the eastern wall and a rough wooden staircase—heavy planks on an uneven frame with one warped unpainted banister, the whole covered with a sloping roof of corrugated iron—hung precariously at the back of the house, in striking contrast with the white-pointed brickwork of the front, the white woodwork and the frosted glass of doors and windows.

For this house Mr. Biswas had paid five thousand five hundred dollars.

Mr. Biswas had built two houses of his own and spent much time looking at houses. Yet he was inexperienced. The houses he had built had been crude wooden things in the country, not much better than huts. And during his search for a house he had always assumed new and modern concrete houses, bright with paint, to be beyond him; and he had looked at few. So when he was faced with one which was accessible, with a solid, respectable, modern front, he was immediately dazzled. He had never visited the house when the afternoon sun was on it. He had first gone one afternoon when it was raining, and the next time, when he had taken the children, it was evening.

Of course there were houses to be bought for two thousand and three thousand dollars, on a whole lot, in rising parts of the city. But these houses were old and decaying, with no fences and no conveniences of any sort. Often on one lot there was a conglomeration of two or three miserable houses, with every room of every house let to a separate family who couldn't legally be got out. What a change from those backyards, overrun with chickens and children, to the drawing room of the solicitor's clerk who, coatless, tieless and in slippers, looked relaxed and comfortable in his morris chair, while the heavy red curtains, reflecting on the polished floor, made the scene as cozy and rich as something in an advertisement! What a change from the Tulsi house!

The solicitor's clerk lived in every house he built. While he lived in the house in Sikkim Street he was building another a discreet distance away, at Morvant. He had never married, and lived with his widowed mother, a gracious woman who gave Mr. Biswas tea and cakes which she had baked herself. Between mother and son there was much affection, and this touched Mr. Biswas, whose own mother, neglected by himself, had died five years before in great poverty.

"I can't tell you how sad it make me to leave this house," the solicitor's clerk said, and Mr. Biswas noted that though the man spoke dialect he was obviously educated and used dialect and an exaggerated accent only to express frankness and cordiality. "Really for my mother's sake, man. That is the onliest reason why I have to move. The old queen can't manage the steps." He nodded towards the back of the house, where the staircase was masked by heavy red curtains. "Heart, you see. Could pass away any day."

Shama had disapproved from the first and never gone to see the house. When Mr. Biswas asked her, "Well, what you think?" Shama said, "Think? Me? Since when you start thinking that I could think anything? If I am not good enough to go and see your house, I don't see how I could be good enough to say what I think."

"Ah!" Mr. Biswas said. "Swelling up. Vexed. I bet you would be saying something different if it was your mother who was spending some of her dirty money to buy this house."

Shama sighed.

"Eh? You could only be happy if we just keep on living with your mother and the rest of your big, happy family. Eh?"

"I don't think anything. *You* have the money, *you* want to buy house, and *I* don't have to think anything."

The news that Mr. Biswas was negotiating for a house of his own had gone around Shama's family. Suniti, a niece of twenty-seven, married, with two children, and abandoned for long periods by her husband, a handsome idler who looked after the railway buildings at Pokima Halt where trains stopped twice a day, Suniti said to Shama, "I hear that you come like a big-shot, Aunt." She didn't hide her amusement. "Buying house and thing."

"Yes, child," Shama said, in her martyr's way.

The exchange took place on the back steps and reached the ears of Mr. Biswas, lying in pants and vest on the Slumber-king bed in the room which contained most of the possessions he had gathered after forty-one years. He had carried on a war with Suniti ever since she was a child, but his contempt had never been able to quell her sarcasm. "Shama," he shouted, "tell that girl to go back and help that worthless husband of hers to look after their goats at Pokima Halt."

The goats were an invention of Mr. Biswas which never failed to irritate Suniti. "Goats!" she said to the yard, and sucked her teeth. "Well, some people at least have goats. Which is more than I could say for some other people."

"Tcha!" Mr. Biswas said softly; and, refusing to be drawn into an argument with Suniti, he turned on his side and continued to read the *Meditations* of Marcus Aurelius.

The very day the house was bought they began to see flaws in it. The staircase was dangerous; the upper floor sagged; there was no back door; most of the windows didn't close; one door could not open; the celotex panels under the eaves had fallen out and left gaps between which bats could enter the attic. They discussed these things as calmly as they could and took care not to express their disappointment openly. And it was astonishing how quickly this disappointment had faded, how quickly they had accommodated themselves to every peculiarity and awkwardness of the house. And once that had happened their eyes ceased to be critical, and the house became simply their house.

When Mr. Biswas came back from the hospital for the first time, he found that the house had been prepared for him. The small garden had been made tidy, the downstairs walls distempered. The Prefect motorcar was in the garage, driven there weeks before from the *Sentinel* office by a friend. The hospital had been a void. He had stepped from that into a welcoming world, a new, ready-made world. He could not quite believe that he had made that world. He could not see why he should have a place in it. And everything by which he was surrounded was examined and rediscovered, with pleasure, surprise, disbelief. Every relationship, every possession.

The kitchen safe. That was more than twenty years old. Shortly after his marriage he had bought it, white and new, from the carpenter at Arwacas, the netting unpainted, the wood still odorous; then, and for some time afterwards, sawdust stuck to your hand when you passed it along the shelves. How often he had stained and varnished it! And painted it too. Patches of the netting were clogged, and varnish and paint had made a thick uneven skin on the woodwork. And in what colors he had painted it! Blue and green and even black. In 1938, the week the Pope died and the *Sentinel* came out with a black border, he had come across a large tin of yellow paint and painted everything yellow, even the typewriter. That had been acquired when, at the age of thirty-three, he had decided to become rich by writing for American and English magazines; a brief, happy, hopeful period. The typewriter had remained idle and yellow, and its color had long since ceased to startle. And why, except that it had moved everywhere with them and they regarded it as one of their possessions, had they kept the hat rack, its glass now leprous, most of its hooks broken, its woodwork ugly with painting-over? The bookcase had been made at Shorthills by an out-of-work black-smith who had been employed by the Tulsis as a cabinet-maker; he revealed his skill in his original craft in every bit of wood he had fashioned, every joint he had made, every ornament he had attempted. And the dining table: bought cheaply from a Deserving Destitute who had got some money from the *Sentinel*'s Deserving Destitutes Fund and wished to show his gratitude to Mr. Biswas. And the Slumber-king bed, where he could no longer sleep because it was upstairs and he had been forbidden to climb steps. And the glass cabinet: bought to please Shama, still dainty, and still practically empty. And the morris suite: the last acquisition, it had belonged to the solicitor's clerk and had been left by him as a gift. And in the garage outside, the Prefect.

But bigger than them all was the house, his house.

How terrible it would have been, at this time, to be without it: to have died among the Tulsis, amid the squalor of that large, disintegrating and indifferent family; to have left Shama and the children among them, in one room; worse, to have lived without even attempting to lay claim to one's portion of the earth; to have lived and died as one had been born, unnecessary and unaccommodated.

Chapter One

from A HOUSE FOR MR. BISWAS

Pastoral

Shortly before he was born there had been another quarrel between Mr. Biswas's mother Bipti and his father Raghu, and Bipti had taken her three children and walked all the way in the hot sun to the village where her mother Bissoondaye lived. There Bipti had cried and told the old story of Raghu's miserliness: how he kept a check on every cent he gave her, counted every biscuit in the tin, and how he would walk ten miles rather than pay a cart a penny.

Bipti's father, futile with asthma, propped himself up on his string bed and said, as he always did on unhappy occasions, "Fate. There is nothing we can do about it."

No one paid him any attention. Fate had brought him from India to the sugar-estate, aged him quickly and left him to die in a crumbling mud hut in the swamplands; yet he spoke of Fate often and affectionately, as though, merely by surviving, he had been particularly favored.

While the old man talked on, Bissoondaye sent for the midwife, made a meal for Bipti's children and prepared beds for them. When the midwife came the children were asleep. Some time later they were awakened by the screams of Mr. Biswas and the shrieks of the midwife.

"What is it?" the old man asked. "Boy or girl?"

"Boy, boy," the midwife cried. "But what sort of boy? Six-fingered, and born in the wrong way."

The old man groaned and Bissoondaye said, "I knew it. There is no luck for me."

At once, though it was night and the way was lonely, she left the hut and walked to the next village, where there was a hedge of cactus. She brought back leaves of cactus, cut them into strips and hung a strip over every door, every window, every aperture through which an evil spirit might enter the hut.

But the midwife said, "Whatever you do, this boy will eat up his own mother and father."

The next morning, when in the bright light it seemed that all evil spirits had surely left the earth, the pundit came, a small, thin man with a sharp satirical face and a dismissing manner. Bissoondaye seated him on the string bed, from which the old man had been turned out, and told him what had happened.

"Hm. Born in the wrong way. At midnight, you said."

Bissoondaye had no means of telling the time, but both she and the midwife had assumed that it was midnight, the inauspicious hour.

Abruptly, as Bissoondaye sat before him with bowed and covered head, the pundit brightened, "Oh, well. It doesn't matter. There are always ways and means of getting over these unhappy things." He undid his red bundle and took out his astrological almanac, a sheaf of loose thick leaves, long and narrow, between boards. The leaves were brown with age and their musty smell was mixed with that of the red and ochre sandalwood paste that had been spattered on them. The pundit lifted a leaf, read a little, wet his forefinger on his tongue and lifted another leaf.

At last he said, "First of all, the features of this unfortunate boy. He will have good teeth but they will be rather wide, and there will be spaces between them. I suppose you know what that means. The boy will be a lecher and a spendthrift. Possibly a liar as well. It is hard to be sure about those gaps between the teeth. They might mean only one of those things or they might mean all three."

"What about the six fingers, pundit?"

"That's a shocking sign, of course. The only thing I can advise is to keep him away from trees and water. Particularly water."

"Never bathe him?"

"I don't mean exactly that." He raised his right hand,

bunched the fingers and, with his head on one side, said slowly, "One has to interpret what the book says." He tapped the wobbly almanac with his left hand. "And when the book says water, I think it means water in its natural form."

"Natural form."

"Natural form," the pundit repeated, but uncertainly. "I mean," he said quickly, and with some annoyance, "keep him away from rivers and ponds. And of course the sea. And another thing," he added with satisfaction. "He will have an unlucky sneeze." He began to pack the long leaves of his almanac. "Much of the evil this boy will undoubtedly bring will be mitigated if his father is forbidden to see him for twenty-one days."

"That will be easy," Bissoondaye said, speaking with emotion for the first time.

"On the twenty-first day the father *must* see the boy. But not in the flesh."

"In a mirror, pundit?"

"I would consider that ill-advised. Use a brass plate. Scour it well."

"Of course."

"You must fill this brass plate with coconut oil—which, by the way, you must make yourself from coconuts you have collected with your own hands—and in the reflection on this oil the father must see his son's face." He tied the almanac together and rolled it in the red cotton wrapper which was also spattered with sandalwood paste. "I believe that is all."

"We forgot one thing, punditji. The name."

"I can't help you completely there. But it seems to me that a perfectly safe prefix would be *Mo.* It is up to you to think of something to add to that."

"Oh, punditji, you must help me. I can only think of *hun.*"

The pundit was surprised and genuinely pleased. "But that is excellent. Excellent. *Mohun.* I couldn't have chosen better myself. For Mohun, as you know, means the beloved, and was the name given by the milkmaids to Lord Krishna." His eyes softened at the thought of the legend and for a moment he appeared to forget Bissoondaye and Mr. Biswas.

From the knot at the end of her veil Bissoondaye took out a florin and offered it to the pundit, mumbling her regret that she could not give more. The pundit said that she had done her best and was not to worry. In fact he was pleased; he had expected less.

Mr. Biswas lost his sixth finger before he was nine days old. It simply came off one night and Bipti had an unpleasant turn when, shaking out the sheets one morning, she saw this tiny finger tumble to the ground. Bissoondaye thought this an excellent sign and buried the finger behind the cowpen at the back of the house, not far from where she had buried Mr. Biswas's navel-string.

In the days that followed Mr. Biswas was treated with attention and respect. His brothers and sisters were slapped if they disturbed his sleep, and the flexibility of his limbs was regarded as a matter of importance. Morning and evening he was massaged with coconut oil. All his joints were exercised; his arms and legs were folded diagonally across his red shining body; the big toe of his right foot was made to touch his left shoulder, the big toe of his left foot was made to touch his right shoulder, and both toes were made to touch his nose; finally, all his limbs were bunched together over his belly and then, with a clap and a laugh, released.

Mr. Biswas responded well to these exercises, and Bissoondaye became so confident that she decided to have a celebration on the ninth day. She invited people from the village and fed them. The pundit came and was unexpectedly gracious, though his manner suggested that but for his intervention there would have been no celebration at all. Jhagru, the barber, brought his drum, and Selochan did the Shiva dance in the cowpen, his body smeared all over with ash.

There was an unpleasant moment when Raghu, Mr. Biswas's father, appeared. He had walked; his dhoti and jacket were sweated and dusty. "Well, this is very nice," he said. "Celebrating. And where is the father?"

"Leave this house at once," Bissoondaye said, coming out of the kitchen at the side. "Father! What sort of father do you call yourself, when you drive your wife away every time she gets heavy-footed?"

"That is none of your business," Raghu said. "Where is my son?"

"Go ahead. God has paid you back for your boasting and your meanness. Go and see your son. He will eat you up. Six-fingered, born in the wrong way. Go in and see him. He has an unlucky sneeze as well."

Raghu halted. "Unlucky sneeze?"

"I have warned you. You can only see him on the twenty-first day. If you do anything stupid now the responsibility will be yours."

From his string bed the old man muttered abuse at Raghu. "Shameless, wicked. When I see the behavior of this man I begin to feel that the Black Age has come."

The subsequent quarrel and threats cleared the air. Raghu confessed he had been in the wrong and had already suffered much for it. Bipti said she was willing to go back to him. And he agreed to come again on the twenty-first day.

To prepare for that day Bissoondaye began collecting dry coconuts. She husked them, grated the kernels and set about extracting the oil the pundit had prescribed. It was a long job of boiling and skimming and boiling again, and it was surprising how many coconuts it took to make a little oil. But the oil was ready in time, and Raghu came, neatly dressed, his hair plastered flat and shining, his moustache trimmed, and he was very correct as he took off his hat and went into the dark inner room of the hut which smelled warmly of oil and old thatch. He held his hat on the right side of his face and looked down into the oil in the brass plate. Mr. Biswas, hidden from his father by the hat, and well wrapped from head to foot, was held face downwards over the oil. He didn't like it; he furrowed his forehead, shut his eyes tight and bawled. The oil rippled, clear amber, broke up the reflection of Mr. Biswas's face, already distorted with rage, and the viewing was over.

A few days later Bipti and her children returned home. And there Mr. Biswas's importance steadily diminished. The time came when even the daily massage ceased.

But he still carried weight. They never forgot that he was an unlucky child and that his sneeze was particularly unlucky. Mr. Biswas caught cold easily and in the rainy season threatened his family with destitution. If, before Raghu left for the sugar-estate, Mr. Biswas sneezed, Raghu remained at home, worked on his vegetable garden in the morning and spent the afternoon making walking-sticks and sabots, or carving designs on the hafts of cutlasses and the heads of walking-sticks. His favorite design was a pair of Wellingtons; he had never owned Wellingtons but had seen them on the overseer. Whatever he did, Raghu never left the house. Even so, minor mishaps often followed Mr. Biswas's sneeze: threepence lost in the shopping, the breaking of a bottle, the upsetting of a dish. Once Mr. Biswas sneezed on three mornings in succession.

"This boy will eat up his family in truth," Raghu said.

One morning, just after Raghu had crossed the gutter that ran between the road and his yard, he suddenly stopped. Mr. Biswas had sneezed. Bipti ran out and said, "It doesn't matter. He sneezed when you were already on the road."

"But I heard him. Distinctly."

Bipti persuaded him to go to work. About an hour or two later, while she was cleaning the rice for the midday meal, she heard shouts from the road and went out to find Raghu lying in an ox-cart, his right leg swathed in bloody bandages. He was groaning, not from pain, but from anger. The man who had brought him refused to help him into the yard: Mr. Biswas's sneeze was too well known. Raghu had to limp in leaning on Bipti's shoulder.

"This boy will make us all paupers," Raghu said.

He spoke from a deep fear. Though he saved and made himself and his family go without many things, he never ceased to feel that destitution was very nearly upon him.

The more he hoarded, the more he felt he had to waste and to lose, and the more careful he became.

Every Saturday he lined up with the other laborers outside the estate office to collect his pay. The overseer sat at a little table, on which his khaki cork hat rested, wasteful of space, but a symbol of wealth. On his left sat the Indian clerk, important, stern, precise, with small neat hands that wrote small neat figures in black ink and red ink in the tall ledger. As the clerk entered figures and called out names and amounts in his high, precise voice, the overseer selected coins from the columns of silver and the heaps of copper in front of him, and with greater deliberation extracted notes from the blue one-dollar stacks, the smaller red two-dollar stack and the very shallow green five-dollar stack. Few laborers earned five dollars a week; the notes were there to pay those who were collecting their wives' or husbands' wages as well as their own. Around the overseer's cork hat, and seeming to guard it, there were stiff blue paper bags, neatly serrated at the top, printed with large figures and standing upright from the weight of coin inside them. Clean round perforations gave glimpses of the coin and, Raghu had been told, allowed it to breathe.

These bags fascinated Raghu. He had managed to get a few and after many months and a little cheating—turning a shilling into twelve pennies, for example—he had filled them. Thereafter he had never been able to stop. No one, not even Bipti, knew where he hid these bags; but the word had got around that he buried his money and was possibly the richest man in the village. Such talk alarmed Raghu and, to counter it, he increased his austerities.

Mr. Biswas grew. The limbs that had been massaged and oiled twice a day now remained dusty and muddy and unwashed for days. The malnutrition that had given him the sixth finger of misfortune pursued him now with eczema and sores that swelled and burst and scabbed and burst again, until they stank; his ankles and knees and wrists and elbows were in particular afflicted, and the sores left marks like vaccination scars. Malnutrition gave him the shallowest of chests, the thinnest of limbs; it stunted his growth and gave him a soft rising belly. And yet, perceptibly, he grew. He was never aware of being hungry. It never bothered him that he didn't go to school. Life was unpleasant only because the pundit had forbidden him to go near ponds and rivers. Raghu was an excellent swimmer and Bipti wished him to train Mr. Biswas's brothers. So every Sunday morning Raghu took Pratap and Prasad to swim in a stream not far off, and Mr. Biswas stayed at home, to be bathed by Bipti and have all his sores ripped open by her strong rubbing with the blue soap. But in an hour or two the redness and rawness of the sores had faded, scabs were beginning to form, and

Mr. Biswas was happy again. He played at house with his sister Dehuti. They mixed yellow earth with water and made mud fireplaces; they cooked a few grains of rice in empty condensed milk tins; and, using the tops of tins as baking-stones, they made rotis.

In these amusements Prasad and Pratap took no part. Nine and eleven respectively, they were past such frivolities, and had already begun to work, joyfully cooperating with the estates in breaking the law about the employment of children. They had developed adult mannerisms. They spoke with blades of grass between their teeth; they drank noisily and sighed, passing the back of their hands across their mouths; they ate enormous quantities of rice, patted their bellies and belched; and every Saturday they stood up in line to draw their pay. Their job was to look after the buffaloes that drew the cane-carts. The buffaloes' pleasance was a muddy, cloyingly sweet pool not far from the factory; here, with a dozen other thin-limbed boys, noisy, happy, over-energetic and with a full sense of their importance, Pratap and Prasad moved all day in the mud among the buffaloes. When they came home their legs were caked with the buffalo mud which, on drying, had turned white, so that they looked like the trees in fire stations and police stations which are washed with white lime up to the middle of their trunks.

Much as he wanted to, it was unlikely that Mr. Biswas would have joined his brothers at the buffalo pond when he was of age. There was the pundit's ruling against water; and though it could be argued that mud was not water, and though an accident there might have removed the source of Raghu's anxiety, neither Raghu nor Bipti would have done anything against the pundit's advice. In another two or three years, when he could be trusted with a sickle, Mr. Biswas would be made to join the boys and girls of the grass-gang. Between them and the buffalo boys there were constant disputes, and there was no doubt who were superior. The buffalo boys, with their leggings of white mud, tickling the buffaloes and beating them with sticks, shouting at them and controlling them, exercised power. Whereas the children of the grass-gang, walking briskly along the road single file, their heads practically hidden by tall, wide bundles of wet grass, hardly able to see, and, because of the weight on their heads and the grass over their faces, unable to make more than slurred, brief replies to taunts, were easy objects of ridicule.

And it was to be the grass-gang for Mr. Biswas. Later he would move to the cane fields, to weed and clean and plant and reap; he would be paid by the task and his tasks would be measured out by a driver with a long bamboo rod. And there he would remain. He would never become a driver or a weigher because he wouldn't be able to read. Perhaps, after many years, he might save enough to rent or buy a few acres where he would plant his own canes, which he would sell to the estate at a price fixed by them. But he would achieve this only if he had the strength and optimism of his brother Pratap. For that was what Pratap did. And Pratap, illiterate all his days, was to become richer than Mr. Biswas; he was to have a house of his own, a large, strong, well-built house, years before Mr. Biswas.

But Mr. Biswas never went to work on the estates. Events which were to occur presently led him away from that. They did not lead him to riches, but made it possible for him to console himself in later life with the *Meditations* of Marcus Aurelius, while he rested on the Slumberking bed in the one room which contained most of his possessions.

Dhari, the next-door neighbor, bought a cow in calf, and when the calf was born, Dhari, whose wife went out to work and who had no children of his own, offered Mr. Biswas the job of taking water to the calf during the day, at a penny a week. Raghu and Bipti were pleased.

Mr. Biswas loved the calf, for its big head that looked so insecurely attached to its slender body, for its knobbly shaky legs, its big sad eyes and pink stupid nose. He liked to watch the calf tugging fiercely and sloppily at its mother's udders, its thin legs splayed out, its head almost hidden under its mother's belly. And he did more than take water to the calf. He took it for walks across damp fields of razor grass and along the rutted lanes between the cane fields, anxious to feed it with grass of many sorts and unable to understand why the calf resented being led from one place to another.

It was on one of these walks that Mr. Biswas discovered the stream. It could not be here that Raghu brought Pratap and Prasad to swim: it was too shallow. But it was certainly here that Bipti and Dehuti came on Sunday afternoons to do the washing and returned with their fingers white and pinched. Between clumps of bamboo the stream ran over smooth stones of many sizes and colors, the cool sound of water blending with the rustle of the sharp leaves, the creaks of the tall bamboos when they swayed and their groans when they rubbed against one another.

Mr. Biswas stood in the stream and looked down. The swift movement of the water and the noise made him forget its shallowness, the stones felt slippery, and in a panic he scrambled up to the bank and looked at the water, now harmless again, while the calf stood idle and unhappy beside him, not caring for bamboo leaves.

He continued to go to the forbidden stream. Its delights seemed endless. In a small eddy, dark in the shadow of the bank, he came upon a school of small black fish matching their background so well that they might easily have been mistaken for weeds. He lay down on the bamboo leaves and stretched out a hand slowly, but as soon as his fingers touched the water, the fish, with a wriggle and flick, were away. After that, when he saw the fish, he did not try to catch them. He would watch them and then drop things on the water. A dry bamboo leaf might cause a slight tremor among the fish; a bamboo twig might frighten them more; but if he remained still after that and dropped nothing the fish would become calm again. Then he would spit. Though he couldn't spit as well as his brother Pratap who, with casual violence, could make his spit resound wherever it fell, it pleased Mr. Biswas to see his spit circling slowly above the black fish before being carried away into the main stream. Fishing he sometimes tried, with a thin bamboo rod, a length of string, a bent pin and no bait. The fish didn't bite; but if he wiggled the string violently they became frightened. When he had gazed at the fish long enough he dropped a stick into the water; it was good then to see the whole school instantly streaking away.

Then one day Mr. Biswas lost the calf. He had forgotten it, watching the fish. And when, after dropping the stick and scattering the fish, he remembered the calf, it had gone. He hunted for it along the banks and in the adjoining fields. He went back to the field where Dhari had left the calf that morning. The iron picket, its head squashed and shiny from repeated poundings, was there, but no rope was attached to it, no calf. He spent a long time searching, in fields full of tall weeds with fluffy heads, in the gutters, like neat red gashes, between the fields, and among the sugarcane. He called for it, mooing softly so as not to attract the attention of people.

Abruptly, he decided that the calf was lost for good; that the calf was anyway able to look after itself and would somehow make its way back to its mother in Dhari's yard. In the meantime the best thing for him to do would be to hide until the calf was found, or perhaps forgotten. It was getting late and he decided that the best place for him to hide would be at home.

The afternoon was almost over. In the west the sky was gold and smoke. Most of the villagers were back from work, and Mr. Biswas had to make his way home with caution, keeping close to hedges and sometimes hiding in gutters. Unseen, he came right up to the back boundary of their lot. On a stand between the hut and the cowpen he saw Bipti washing enamel, brass and tin dishes with ashes and water. He hid behind the hibiscus hedge. Pratap and Prasad came, blades of grass between their teeth, their close-fitting felt hats damp with sweat, their faces scorched by the sun and stained with sweat, their legs cased in white mud. Pratap threw a length of white cotton around his dirty trousers and undressed with expert adult modesty before using the calabash to throw water over himself from the big black oil barrel. Prasad stood on a board and began scraping the white mud off his legs.

Bipti said, "You boys will have to go and get some wood before it gets dark."

Prasad lost his temper; and, as though by scraping off the white mud he had lost the composure of adulthood, he flung his hat to the ground and cried like a child, "Why do you ask me *now*? Why do you ask me *every* day? I am not going."

Raghu came to the back, an unfinished walking-stick in one hand and in the other a smoking wire with which he had been burning patterns into the stick. "Listen, boy," Raghu said. "Don't feel that because you are earning money you are a man. Do what your mother asks. And go quickly, before I use this stick on you, even though it is unfinished." He smiled at his joke.

Mr. Biswas became uneasy.

Prasad, still raging, picked up his hat, and he and Pratap went away to the front of the house.

Bipti took her dishes to the kitchen in the front veran-dah, where Dehuti would be helping with the evening meal. Raghu went back to his bonfire at the front. Mr. Biswas slipped through the hibiscus fence, crossed the narrow, shallow gutter, gray-black and squelchy with the ashy water from the washing-up stand and the muddy water from Pratap's bath, and made his way to the small back verandah where there was a table, the only piece of carpenter-built furniture in the hut. From the verandah he went into his father's room, passed under the valance

of the bed—planks resting on upright logs sunk into the
earth floor—and prepared to wait.

It was a long wait but he endured it without discom-
fort. Below the bed the smell of old cloth, dust and old
thatch combined into one overpoweringly musty smell.
Idly, to pass the time, he tried to disentangle one smell
from the other, while his ears picked up the sounds in and
around the hut. They were remote and dramatic. He heard
the boys return and throw down the dry wood they had
brought. Prasad still raged, Raghu warned, Bipti coaxed.
Then all at once Mr. Biswas became alert.

"Ey, Raghu?" He recognized Dhari's voice. "Where is
that youngest son of yours?"

"Mohun? Bipti, where is Mohun?"

"With Dhari's calf, I suppose."

"Well, he isn't," Dhari said.

"Prasad!" Bipti called. "Pratap! Dehuti! Have you seen
Mohun?"

"No, mai."

"No, mai."

"No, mai."

"No, mai. No, mai. No, mai," Raghu said. "What the
hell do you think it is? Go and look for him."

"Oh *God*!" Prasad cried.

"And you too, Dhari. It was your idea, getting Mohun
to look after the calf. I hold you responsible."

"The magistrate will have something else to say," Dhari said. "A calf is a calf, and for one who is not as rich as yourself—"

"I am sure nothing has happened," Bipti said. "Mohun knows he mustn't go near water."

Mr. Biswas was startled by a sound of wailing. It came from Dhari. "Water, water. Oh, the unlucky boy. Not content with eating up his mother and father, he is eating me up as well. Water! Oh, Mohun's mother, what you have said?"

"Water?" Raghu sounded puzzled.

"The pond, the pond," Dhari wailed, and Mr. Biswas heard him shouting to the neighbors, "Raghu's son has drowned my calf in the pond. A nice calf. My first calf. My only calf."

Quickly a chattering crowd gathered. Many of them had been to the pond that afternoon; quite a number had seen a calf wandering about, and one or two had even seen a boy.

"Nonsense!" Raghu said. "You are a pack of liars. The boy doesn't go near water." He paused and added, "The pundit especially forbade him to go near water in its natural form."

Lakhan the carter said, "But this is a fine man. He doesn't seem to care whether his son is drowned or not."

"How do you know what he thinks?" Bipti said.

"Leave him, leave him," Raghu said, in an injured, forgiving tone. "Mohun is *my* son. And if I don't care whether he is drowned or not, that is *my* business."

"What about my calf?" Dhari said.

"I don't care about your calf. Pratap! Prasad! Dehuti! Have you seen your brother?"

"No, father."

"No, father."

"No, father."

"I will go and dive for him," Lakhan said.

"You are *very* anxious to show off," Raghu said.

"Oh!" Bipti cried. "Stop this bickering-ickering and let us go to look for the boy."

"Mohun is *my* son," Raghu said. "And if anybody is going to dive for him, it will be me. And I pray to God, Dhari, that when I get to the bottom of that pond I find your wretched calf."

"Witnesses!" Dhari said. "You are all my witnesses. Those words will have to be repeated in court."

"To the pond! To the pond!" the villagers said, and the news was shouted to those just arriving: "Raghu is going to dive for his son in the pond."

Mr. Biswas, under his father's bed, had listened at first with pleasure, then with apprehension. Raghu came into the room, breathing heavily and swearing at the village. Mr. Biswas heard him undress and shout for Bipti to come and rub him down with coconut oil. She came and rubbed him down and they both left the room. From the road chatter and the sound of footsteps rose, and slowly faded.

Mr. Biswas came out from under the bed and was dismayed to find that the hut was dark. In the next room someone began to cry. He went to the doorway and looked. It was Dehuti. From the nail on the wall she had taken down his shirt and two vests and was pressing them to her face.

"Sister," he whispered.

She heard and saw, and her sobs turned to screams.

Mr. Biswas didn't know what to do. "It's all right, it's all right," he said, but the words were useless, and he went back to his father's room. Just in time, for at that moment Sadhu, the very old man who lived two houses away, came and asked what was wrong, his words whistling through the gaps in his teeth.

Dehuti continued to scream. Mr. Biswas put his hands into his trouser pockets and, through the holes in them, pressed his fingers on his thighs.

Sadhu led Dehuti away.

Outside, from an unknown direction, a frog honked, then made a sucking, bubbling noise. The crickets were already chirping. Mr. Biswas was alone in the dark hut, and frightened.

———

The pond lay in swampland. Weeds grew all over its surface and from a distance it appeared to be no more than a shallow depression. In fact it was full of abrupt depths and the villagers liked to think that these were immeasurable. There were no trees or hills around, so that though the sun had gone, the sky remained high and light. The villagers stood silently around the safe edge of the pond. The frogs honked and the poor-me-one bird began to say the mournful words that gave it its name. The mosquitoes were already active; from time to time a villager slapped his arm or lifted a leg and slapped that.

Lakhan the carter said, "He's been down there too long."

Bipti frowned.

Before Lakhan could take off his shirt Raghu broke the surface, puffed out his cheeks, spat out a long thin arc of water and took deep resounding breaths. The water rolled off his oiled skin, but his moustache had collapsed over his upper lip and his hair fell in a fringe over his forehead. Lakhan gave him a hand up. "I believe there is something down there," Raghu said. "But it is very dark."

Far away the low trees were black against the fading sky; the orange streaks of sunset were smudged with gray, as if by dirty thumbs.

Bipti said, "Let Lakhan dive."

Someone else said, "Leave it till tomorrow."

"Till tomorrow?" Raghu said. "And poison the water for everybody?"

Lakhan said, "I will go."

Raghu, panting, shook his head. "*My* son. *My* duty."

"And my calf," Dhari said.

Raghu ignored him. He ran his hands through his hair, puffed out his cheeks, put his hands to his sides and belched. In a moment he was in the water again. The pond didn't permit stylish diving; Raghu merely let himself down. The water broke and rippled. The gleam it got from the sky was fading. While they waited a cool wind came down from the hills to the north; between the shaking weeds the water shimmered like sequins.

Lakhan said, "He's coming up now. I believe he's got something."

They knew what it was from Dhari's cry. Then Bipti began to scream, and Pratap and Prasad and all the women, while the men helped to lift the calf to the bank. One of its sides was green with slime; its thin limbs were ringed with vinelike weeds, still fresh and thick and green. Raghu sat on the bank, looking down between his legs at the dark water.

Lakhan said, "Let me go down now and look for the boy."

"Yes, man," Bipti pleaded. "Let him go."

Raghu remained where he was, breathing deeply, his

dhoti clinging to his skin. Then he was in the water and the villagers were silent again. They waited, looking at the calf, looking at the pond.

Lakhan said, "Something has happened."

A woman said, "No stupid talk now, Lakhan. Raghu is a great diver."

"I know, I know," Lakhan said. "But he's been diving too long."

Then they were all still. Someone had sneezed.

They turned to see Mr. Biswas standing some distance away in the gloom, the toe of one foot scratching the ankle of the other.

Lakhan was in the pond. Pratap and Prasad rushed to hustle Mr. Biswas away.

"That boy!" Dhari said. "He has murdered my calf and now he has eaten up his own father."

Lakhan brought up Raghu unconscious. They rolled him on the damp grass and pumped water out of his mouth and through his nostrils. But it was too late.

"Messages," Bipti kept on saying. "We must send messages." And messages were taken everywhere by willing and excited villagers. The most important message went to Bipti's sister Tara at Pagotes. Tara was a person of standing. It was her fate to be childless, but it was also her fate to have married a man who had, at one bound, freed himself from the land and acquired wealth; already he owned a rumshop and a dry goods shop, and he had been one of the first in Trinidad to buy a motorcar.

Tara came and at once took control. Her arms were encased from wrist to elbow with silver bangles which she had often recommended to Bipti: "They are not very pretty, but one clout from this arm will settle any attacker." She also wore earrings and a *nakphul,* a "nose-flower." She had a solid gold yoke around her neck and thick silver bracelets on her ankles. In spite of all her jewelry she was energetic and capable, and had adopted her husband's commanding manner. She left the mourning to Bipti and arranged everything else. She had brought her own pundit, whom she continually harangued; she instructed Pratap how to behave during the ceremonies; and she had even brought a photographer.

She urged Prasad, Dehuti and Mr. Biswas to behave with dignity and to keep out of the way, and she ordered Dehuti to see that Mr. Biswas was properly dressed. As the baby of the family Mr. Biswas was treated by the mourners with honor and sympathy, though this was touched with a little dread. Embarrassed by their attentions, he moved about the hut and yard, thinking he could detect a new, raw smell in the air. There was also a strange taste in his mouth; he had never eaten meat, but now he felt he had eaten raw white flesh; nauseating saliva rose continually at the back of his throat and he had to keep on spitting, until Tara said, "What's the matter with you? Are you pregnant?"

Bipti was bathed. Her hair, still wet, was neatly parted and the parting filled with red henna. Then the henna was scooped out and the parting filled with charcoal dust. She was now a widow forever. Tara gave a short scream and at her signal the other women began to wail. On Bipti's wet black hair there were still spots of henna, like drops of blood.

Cremation was forbidden and Raghu was to be buried. He lay in a coffin in the bedroom, dressed in his finest dhoti, jacket and turban, his beads around his neck and down his jacket. The coffin was strewn with marigolds which matched his turban. Pratap, the eldest son, did the last rites, walking round the coffin.

"Photo now," Tara said. "Quick. Get them all together. For the last time."

The photograper, who had been smoking under the mango tree, went into the hut and said, "Too dark."

The men became interested and gave advice while the women wailed.

"Take it outside. Lean it against the mango tree."

"Light a lamp."

"It *couldn't* be too dark."

"What do you know? You've never had your photo taken. Now, what *I* suggest—"

The photographer, of mixed Chinese, Negro and European blood, did not understand what was being said. In the end he and some of the men took the coffin out to the verandah and stood it against the wall.

"Careful! Don't let him fall out."

"Goodness. All the marigolds have dropped out."

"Leave them," the photographer said in English. "Is a nice little touch. Flowers on the ground." He set up his tripod in the yard, just under the ragged eaves of thatch, and put his head under the black cloth.

Tara roused Bipti from her grief, arranged Bipti's hair and veil, and dried Bipti's eyes.

"Five people all together," the photographer said to Tara. "Hard to know just how to arrange them. It look to me that it would have to be two one side and three the other side. You sure you want all five?"

Tara was firm.

The photographer sucked his teeth, but not at Tara. "Look, look. Why nobody ain't put anything to chock up the coffin and prevent it from slipping?"

Tara had that attended to.

The photographer said, "All right then. Mother and biggest son on either side. Next to mother, young boy and young girl. Next to big son, smaller son."

There was more advice from the men.

"Make them look at the coffin."

"At the mother."

"At the youngest boy."

The photographer settled the matter by telling Tara, "Tell them to look at me."

Tara translated, and the photographer went under his cloth. Almost immediately he came out again. "How about making the mother and the biggest boy put their hands on the edge of the coffin?"

This was done and the photographer went back under his cloth.

"Wait!" Tara cried, running out from the hut with a fresh garland of marigolds. She hung it around Raghu's neck and said to the photographer in English, "All right. Draw your photo now."

Mr. Biswas never owned a copy of the photograph and he did not see it until 1937, when it made its appearance, framed in passe-partout, on the wall of the drawing room of Tara's fine new house at Pagotes, a little lost among many other photographs of funeral groups, many oval portraits with blurred edges of more dead friends and relations and colored prints of the English countryside. The photograph had faded to the lightest brown and was partially defaced by the large heliotrope stamp of the photographer, still bright, and his smudged sprawling signature in soft black pencil. Mr. Biswas was astonished at his own smallness. The scabs of sores and the marks of eczema showed clearly on his knobbly knees and along his very thin arms and legs. Everyone in the photograph had unnaturally large, staring eyes which seemed to have been outlined in black.

Tara was right when she said that the photograph was to be a record of the family all together for the last time. For in a few days Mr. Biswas and Bipti, Pratap and Prasad and Dehuti had left Parrot Trace and the family split up for good.

It began on the evening of the funeral.

Tara said, "Bipti, you must give me Dehuti."

Bipti had been hoping that Tara would make the suggestion. In four or five years Dehuti would have to be married and it was better that she should be given to Tara. She would learn manners, acquire graces and, with a dowry from Tara, might even make a good match.

"If you are going to have someone," Tara said, "it is better to have one of your own family. That is what I always say. I don't want strangers poking their noses into my kitchen and bedroom."

Bipti agreed that it was better to have servants from one's own family. And Pratap and Prasad and even Mr. Biswas, who had not been asked, nodded, as though the problem of servants was one they had given much thought.

Dehuti looked down at the floor, shook her long hair and mumbled a few words which meant that she was far too small to be consulted, but was very pleased.

"Get her new clothes," Tara said, fingering the georgette skirt and satin petticoat Dehuti had worn for the funeral. "Get her some jewels." She put a thumb and finger around Dehuti's wrist, lifted her face and turned up the lobe of her ear. "Earrings. Good thing you had them pierced, Bipti. She won't need these sticks now." In the holes in her lobe Dehuti wore pieces of the thin hard spine of the blades of the coconut branch. Tara playfully pulled Dehuti's nose. "*Nakphul* too. You would like a nose-flower?"

Dehuti smiled shyly, not looking up.

"Well," Tara said, "fashions are changing all the time these days. I am just old-fashioned, that is all." She stroked her gold nose-flower. "It is expensive to be old-fashioned."

"She will satisfy you," Bipti said. "Raghu had no money. But he trained his children well. Training, piety—"

"Quite," Tara said. "The time for crying is over, Bipti. How much money did Raghu leave you?"

"Nothing. I don't know."

"What do you mean? Are you trying to keep secrets from me? Everyone in the village knows that Raghu had a lot of money. I am sure he has left you enough to start a nice little business."

Pratap sucked his teeth. "He was a miser, that one. He used to hide his money."

Tara said, "Is this the training and piety your father gave you?"

They searched. They pulled out Raghu's box from under the bed and looked for false bottoms; at Bipti's suggestion they looked for any joint that might reveal a hiding-place in the timber itself. They poked the sooty thatch and ran their hands over the rafters; they tapped the earth floor and the bamboo-and-mud walls; they examined Raghu's walking-sticks, taking out the ferrules, Raghu's only extravagance; they dismantled the bed and uprooted the logs on which it stood. They found nothing.

Bipti said, "I don't suppose he had any money really."

"You are a fool," Tara said, and it was in this mood of annoyance that she ordered Bipti to pack Dehuti's bundle and took Dehuti away.

Because no cooking could be done at their house, they ate at Sadhu's. The food was unsalted and as soon as he began to chew, Mr. Biswas felt he was eating raw flesh and the nauseous saliva filled his mouth again. He hurried outside to empty his mouth and clean it, but the taste remained. And Mr. Biswas screamed when, back at the hut, Bipti put him to bed and threw Raghu's blanket over him. The

blanket was hairy and prickly; it seemed to be the source
of the raw, fresh smell he had been smelling all day. Bipti
let him scream until he was tired and fell asleep in the yellow, wavering light of the oil lamp which left the corners
in darkness. She watched the wick burn lower and lower
until she heard the snores of Pratap, who snored like a big
man, and the heavy breathing of Mr. Biswas and Prasad.
She slept only fitfully herself. It was quiet inside the hut,
but outside the noises were loud and continuous: mosquitoes, bats, frogs, crickets, the poor-me-one. If the cricket
missed a chirp the effect was disturbing and she awoke.

She was awakened from a light sleep by a new noise. At
first she couldn't be sure. But the nearness of the noise and
its erratic sequence disturbed her. It was a noise she heard
every day but now, isolated in the night, it was hard to place.
It came again: a thud, a pause, a prolonged snapping, then
a series of gentler thuds. And it came again. Then there was
another noise, of bottles breaking, muffled, as though the
bottles were full. And she knew the noises came from her
garden. Someone was stumbling among the bottles Raghu
had buried neck downwards around the flower-beds.

She roused Prasad and Pratap.

Mr. Biswas, awaking to hushed talk and a room of
dancing shadows, closed his eyes to keep out the danger;
at once, as on the day before, everything became dramatic
and remote.

Pratap gave walking-sticks to Prasad and Bipti. Carefully he unbolted the small window, then pushed it out with sudden vigor.

The garden was lit up by a hurricane lamp. A man was working a fork into the ground among the bottle-borders.

"Dhari!" Bipti called.

Dhari didn't look up or reply. He went on forking, rocking the implement in the earth, tearing the roots that kept the earth firm.

"Dhari!"

He began to sing a wedding song.

"The cutlass!" Pratap said. "Give me the cutlass."

"O God! No, no," Bipti said.

"I'll go out and beat him like a snake," Pratap said, his voice rising out of control. "Prasad? Mai?"

"Close the window," Bipti said.

The singing stopped and Dhari said, "Yes, close the window and go to sleep. I am here to look after you."

Violently Bipti pulled the small window to, bolted it and kept her hand on the bolt.

The digging and the breaking bottles continued. Dhari sang:

> *In your daily tasks be resolute.*
> *Fear no one, and trust in God.*

"Dhari isn't in this alone," Bipti said. "Don't provoke him." Then, as though it not only belittled Dhari's behavior but gave protection to them all, she added, "He is only after your father's money. Let him look."

Mr. Biswas and Prasad were soon asleep again. Bipti and Pratap remained up until they had heard the last of Dhari's songs and his fork no longer dug into the earth and broke bottles. They did not speak. Only, once, Bipti said, "Your father always warned me about the people of this village."

Pratap and Prasad awoke when it was still dark, as they always did. They did not talk about what had happened and Bipti insisted that they should go to the buffalo pond as usual. As soon as it was light she went out to the garden. The flower-beds had been dug up; dew lay on the upturned earth which partially buried uprooted plants, already limp and quailing. The vegetable patch had not been forked, but tomato plants had been cut down, stakes broken and pumpkins slashed.

"Oh, wife of Raghu!" a man called from the road, and she saw Dhari jump across the gutter.

Absently, he picked a dew-wet leaf from the hibiscus shrub, crushed it in his palm, put it in his mouth and came towards her, chewing.

Her anger rose. "Get out! At once! Do you call yourself a man? You are a shameless vagabond. Shameless and cowardly."

He walked past her, past the hut, to the garden. Chewing, he considered the damage. He was in his working clothes, his cutlass in its black leather sheath at his waist, his enamel food-carrier in one hand, his calabash of water hanging from his shoulder.

"Oh, wife of Raghu, what have they done?"

"I hope you found something to make you happy, Dhari."

He shrugged, looking down at the ruined flower-beds. "They will keep on looking, *maharajin*."

"Everybody knows you lost your calf. But that was an accident. What about—"

"Yes, yes. My calf. Accident."

"I will remember you for this, Dhari. And Raghu's sons won't forget you either."

"He was a great diver."

"Savage! Get out!"

"Willingly." He spat out the hibiscus leaf on to a flower-bed. "I just wanted to tell you that these wicked men will come again. Why don't you help them, *maharajin*?"

There was no one Bipti could ask for help. She distrusted the police, and Raghu had no friends. Moreover, she didn't know who might be in league with Dhari.

That night they gathered all Raghu's sticks and cutlasses and waited. Mr. Biswas closed his eyes and listened, but as the hours passed he found it hard to remain alert.

He was awakened by whispers and movement in the hut. Far away, it seemed, someone was singing a slow, sad wedding song. Bipti and Prasad were standing. Cutlass in hand, Pratap moved in a frenzy between the window and the door, so swiftly that the flame of the oil lamp blew this way and that, and once, with a plopping sound, disappeared. The room sank into darkness. A moment later the flame returned, rescuing them.

The singing drew nearer, and when it was almost upon them they heard, mingled with it, chatter and soft laughter.

Bipti unbolted the window, pushed it open a crack, and saw the garden ablaze with lanterns.

"Three of them," she whispered. "Lakhan, Dhari, Oumadh."

Pratap pushed Bipti aside, flung the window wide open and screamed, "Get out! Get out! I will kill you all."

"Shh," Bipti said, pulling Pratap away and trying to close the window.

"Raghu's son," a man said from the garden.

"Don't sh me," Pratap screamed, turning on Bipti. Tears came to his eyes and his voice broke into sobs. "I will kill them all."

"Noisy little fellow," another man said.

"I will come back and kill you all," Pratap shouted. "I promise you."

Bipti took him in her arms and comforted him, like a child, and in the same gentle, unalarmed voice said, "Prasad, close the window. And go to sleep."

"Yes, son." They recognized Dhari's voice. "Go to sleep. We will be here every night now to look after you."

Prasad closed the window, but the noise stayed with them: song, talk and unhurried sounds of fork and spade. Bipti sat and stared at the door, next to which, on the ground, Pratap sat, a cutlass beside him, its haft carved into a pair of wellingtons. He was motionless. His tears had gone, but his eyes were red, and the lids swollen.

In the end Bipti sold the hut and the land to Dhari, and she and Mr. Biswas moved to Pagotes. There they lived on Tara's bounty, though not with Tara, but with some of Tara's husband's dependent relations in a back trace far from the Main Road. Pratap and Prasad were sent to a distant relation at Felicity, in the heart of the sugar-estates; they were already broken into estate work and were too old to learn anything else.

And so Mr. Biswas came to leave the only house to which he had some right. For the next thirty-five years he was to be a wanderer with no place he could call his own, with no family except that which he was to attempt to create out of the engulfing world of the Tulsis. For with his mother's parents dead, his father dead, his brothers on the estate at Felicity, Dehuti as a servant in Tara's house, and himself rapidly growing away from Bipti who, broken, became increasingly useless and impenetrable, it seemed to him that he was really quite alone.

JASMINE

One day about ten years ago, when I was editing a weekly literary program for the BBC's Caribbean Service, a man from Trinidad came to see me in one of the freelances' rooms in the old Langham Hotel. He sat on the edge of the table, slapped down some sheets of typescript and said, "My name is Smith. I write about sex. I am also a nationalist." The sex was tepid, Maugham and coconut-water; but the nationalism was aggressive. Women swayed like coconut trees; their skins were the color of the sapodilla, the inside of their mouths the color of a cut star-apple; their teeth were as white as coconut kernels; and when they made love they groaned like bamboos in high wind.

The writer was protesting against what the English language had imposed on us. The language was ours, to use

as we pleased. The literature that came with it was there-
fore of peculiar authority; but this literature was like an
alien mythology. There was, for instance, Wordsworth's
notorious poem about the daffodil. A pretty little flower,
no doubt; but we had never seen it. Could the poem have
any meaning for us? The superficial prompting of this
argument, which would have confined all literatures to
the countries of their origin, was political; but it was really
an expression of dissatisfaction at the emptiness of our
own formless, unmade society. To us, without a mythology, all literatures were foreign. Trinidad was small, remote
and unimportant, and we knew we could not hope to
read in books of the life we saw about us. Books came
from afar; they could offer only fantasy.

To open a book was to make an instant adjustment.
Like the medieval sculptor of the North interpreting the
Old Testament stories in terms of the life he knew, I
needed to be able to adapt. All Dickens's descriptions of
London I rejected; and though I might retain Mr. Micaw-
ber and the others in the clothes the illustrator gave them,
I gave them the faces and voices of people I knew and set
them in buildings and streets I knew. The process of adaptation was automatic and continuous. Dickens's rain and
drizzle I turned into tropical downpours; the snow and
fog I accepted as conventions of books. Anything—like
an illustration—which embarrassed me by proving how
weird my own recreation was, anything which sought to

remove the characters from the make-up world in which I set them, I rejected.

I went to books for fantasy; at the same time I required reality. The gypsies of *The Mill on the Floss* were a fabrication and a disappointment, discrediting so much that was real: to me gypsies were mythical creatures who belonged to the pure fantasy of Hans Christian Andersen and *The Heroes*. Disappointing, too, was the episode of the old soldier's sword, because I thought that swords belonged to ancient times; and the Tom Tulliver I had created walked down the street where I lived. The early parts of *The Mill on the Floss*, then; chapters of *Oliver Twist, Nicholas Nickleby, David Copperfield*; some of the novels of H. G. Wells; a short story by Conrad called "The Lagoon": all these which in the beginning I read or had read to me I set in Trinidad, accepting, rejecting, adapting and peopling in my own way. I never read to find out about foreign countries. Everything in books was foreign; everything had to be subjected to adaptation; and everything in, say, an English novel which worked and was of value to me at once ceased to be specifically English. Mr. Murdstone worked; Mr. Pickwick and his club didn't. *Jane Eyre* and *Wuthering Heights* worked; *Pride and Prejudice* didn't. Maupassant worked; Balzac didn't.

I went to books for a special sort of participation. The only social division I accepted was that between rich and poor, and any society more elaborately ordered seemed insubstantial and alien. In literature such a society was more than alien; it was excluding, it made nonsense of my fantasies and more and more, as I grew older and thought of writing myself, it made me despairingly conscious of the poverty and haphazardness of my own society. I might adapt Dickens to Trinidad; but it seemed impossible that the life I knew in Trinidad could ever be turned into a book. If landscapes do not start to be real until they have been interpreted by an artist, so, until they have been written about, societies appear to be without shape and *embarrassing*. It was embarrassing to be reminded by a Dickens illustration of the absurdity of my adaptations; it was equally embarrassing to attempt to write of what I saw. Very little of what I read was of help. It would have been possible to assume the sensibility of a particular writer. But no writer, however individual his vision, could be separated from his society. The vision was alien; it diminished my own and did not give me the courage to do a simple thing like mentioning the name of a Port of Spain street.

Fiction or any work of the imagination, whatever its quality, hallows its subject. To attempt, with a full consciousness of established authoritative mythologies, to give a quality of myth to what was agreed to be petty and ridiculous—Frederick Street in Port of Spain, Marine Square, the districts of Laventille and Barataria—to attempt to use these names required courage. It was, in a way, the rejection of the familiar, meaningless word—the rejection of the unknown daffodil to put it no higher—and was as self-conscious as the attempt to have sapodilla-skinned women groaning like bamboos in high wind.

With all English literature accessible, then, my position was like that of the maharaja in *Hindoo Holiday,* who, when told by the Christian lady that God was here, there and everywhere, replied, "But what use is that to *me*?" Something of more pertinent virtue was needed, and this was provided by some local short stories. These stories, perhaps a dozen in all, never published outside Trinidad, converted what I saw into "writing." It was through them that I began to appreciate the distorting, distilling power of the writer's art. Where I had seen a drab haphazardness they found order; where I would have attempted to romanticize, to render my subject equal with what I had read, they accepted. They provided a starting-point for further observation; they did not trigger off fantasy. Every writer is, in the long run, on his own; but it helps, in the most practical way, to have a tradition. The English language was mine; the tradition was not.

Literature, then, was mainly fantasy. Perhaps it was for this reason that, although I had at an early age decided to be a writer and at the age of eighteen had left Trinidad with that ambition, I did not start writing seriously until I was nearly twenty-three. My material had not been sufficiently hallowed by a tradition; I was not fully convinced of its importance; and some embarrassment remained. My taste for literature had developed into a love of language, the word in isolation. At school my subjects were French and Spanish; and the pleasures of the language were at least as great as those of the literature. Maupassant and Molière were rich; but it was more agreeable to spend an hour with the big Harrap French-English dictionary, learning more of the language through examples, than with Corneille or Racine. And it was because I thought I had had enough of these languages (both now grown rusty) that when I came to England to go to university I decided to read English.

This was a mistake. The English course had little to do with literature. It was a "discipline" seemingly aimed at juvenile antiquarians. It bypassed the novel and the prose "asides" in which so much of the richness of the literature lay. By a common and curious consent it concentrated on poetry; and since it stopped at the eighteenth century it degenerated, after an intensive study of Shakespeare, into a lightning survey of minor and often severely local talents. I had looked forward to wandering among large tracts of writing; I was presented with "texts." The metaphysicals were a perfect subject for study, a perfect part of a discipline; but, really, they had no value for me. Dryden, for all the sweet facility of his prose, was shallow and dishonest; did his "criticism" deserve such reverential attention? *Gulliver's Travels* was excellent; but could *The Tale of a Tub* and *The Battle of the Books* be endured?

The fact was, I had no taste for scholarship, for tracing

the growth of schools and trends. I sought continuously to relate literature to life. My training at school didn't help. We had few libraries, few histories of literature to turn to; and when we wrote essays on *Tartuffe* we wrote out of a direct response to the play. Now I discovered that the study of literature had been made scientific, that each writer had to be approached through the booby-traps of scholarship. There were the bound volumes of the Publications of the Modern Language Association of America, affectionately referred to by old and knowing young as PMLA. The pages that told of Chaucer's knowledge of astronomy or astrology (the question came up every year) were black and bloated and furred with handling, and even some of the penciled annotations (*No, Norah!*) had grown faint. I developed a physical distaste for these bound volumes and the libraries that housed them.

Delight cannot be taught and measured; scholarship can; and my reaction was irrational. But it seemed to me scholarship of such a potted order. A literature was not being explored; it had been codified and reduced to a few pages of "text," some volumes of "background" and more of "criticism"; and to this mixture a mathematical intelligence might have been applied. There were discoveries, of course: Shakespeare, Marlowe, Restoration comedy. But my distaste for the study of literature led to a sense of being more removed than ever from the literature itself.

The language remained mine, and it was to the study

of its development that I turned with pleasure. Here was enough to satisfy my love of language; here was unexpected adventure. It might not have been easy to see Chaucer as a great imaginative writer or to find in the *Prologue* more than a limited piece of observation which had been exceeded a thousand times; but Chaucer as a handler of a new, developing language was exciting. And my pleasure in Shakespeare was doubled. In Trinidad English writing had been for me a starting-point for fantasy. Now, after some time in England, it was possible to isolate the word, to separate the literature from the language.

Language can be so deceptive. It has taken me much time to realize how bad I am at interpreting the conventions and modes of English speech. This speech has never been better dissected than in the early stories of Angus Wilson. This is the judgment of today; my first responses to these stories were as blundering and imperfect as the responses of Professor Pforzheim to the stern courtesies of his English colleagues in *Anglo-Saxon Attitudes.* But while knowledge of England has made English writing more truly accessible, it has made participation more difficult; it has made impossible the exercise of fantasy, the reader's complementary response. I am inspecting an alien society, which I yet know, and I am looking for particular social comment. And to re-read now the books which lent themselves to fantastic interpretation in Trinidad is to see, almost with dismay, how English they are. The illustrations to Dickens cannot now be dismissed. And so, with knowledge, the books have ceased to be mine.

It is the English literary vice, this looking for social comment; and it is difficult to resist. The preoccupation of the novelists reflects a society ruled by convention and manners in the fullest sense, an ordered society of the self-aware who read not so much for adventure as to compare, to find what they know or think they know. A writer is to be judged by what he reports on; the working-class writer is a working-class writer and no more. So writing develops into the private language of a particular society. There are new reports, new discoveries: they are rapidly absorbed. And with each discovery the society's image of itself becomes more fixed and the society looks further inward. It has too many points of reference; it has been written about too often; it has read too much. Angus Wilson's characters, for instance, are great readers; they are steeped in Dickens and Jane Austen. Soon there will be characters steeped in Angus Wilson; the process is endless. Sensibility will overlay sensibility: the grossness of experience will be refined away by self-awareness. Writing will become Arthur Miller's definition of a newspaper: a nation talking to itself. And even those who have the key will be able only to witness, not to participate.

All literatures are regional; perhaps it is only the placelessness of a Shakespeare or the blunt communication of "gross" experience as in Dickens that makes them appear less so. Or perhaps it is a lack of knowledge in the reader. Even in this period of "internationalism" in letters we have seen literatures turning more and more inward, developing languages that are more and more private. Perhaps in the end literature will write itself out, and all its pleasures will be those of the word.

A little over three years ago I was in British Guiana. I was taken late one afternoon to meet an elderly lady of a distinguished Christian Indian family. Our political attitudes were too opposed to make any discussion of the current crisis profitable. We talked of the objects in her verandah and of the old days. Suddenly the tropical daylight was gone, and from the garden came the scent of a flower. I knew the flower from my childhood; yet I had never found out its name. I asked now.

"We call it jasmine."

Jasmine! So I had known it all those years! To me it had been a word in a book, a word to play with, something removed from the dull vegetation I knew.

The old lady cut a sprig for me. I stuck it in the top buttonhole of my open shirt. I smelled it as I walked back to the hotel. Jasmine, jasmine. But the word and the flower had been separate in my mind for too long. They did not come together.

SYNTHESIS AND MIMICRY

1

At a dinner party in Delhi, a young foreign academic, describing what was most noticeable about the crowds he had seen in Bombay on his Indian holiday, said with a giggle: "They were doing their 'potties' on the street." He was adding to what his Indian wife had said with mystical gravity: she saw people only having their being. She was middle-class and well connected. He was shallow and brisk and common, enjoying his pickings, swinging happily from branch to low branch in the grove of Academe. But the couple were well matched in an important way. Her Indian blindness to India, with its roots in caste and religion, was like his foreigner's easy disregard. The combination is not new; it has occurred again and again in the last thousand years of Indian history, the understanding based on Indian misunderstanding; and India has always been the victim.

But this couple lived outside India. They returned from time to time as visitors, and India restored in different ways the self-esteem of each. For other people in that gathering, however, who lived in India and felt the new threat of the millions and all the uncertainties that had come with Independence and growth, India could no longer be taken for granted. The poor had ceased to be background. Another way of looking was felt to be needed, some profounder acknowledgement of the people of the streets.

And this was what was attempted by another young woman, a friend of the couple who lived abroad. The women of Bombay, she said, and she meant the women of the lower castes, wore a certain kind of sari and preferred certain colors; the men wore a special kind of turban. She had lived in Bombay; but, already, she was wrong: it is true that the women dress traditionally, but in Bombay the men for the most part wear trousers and shirt. It was a revealing error: for all her sympathy with the poor, she was still receptive only to caste signals, and was as blind as her friend.

"I will tell you about the poor people in Bombay," she insisted. "They are beautiful. They are more beautiful than the people in this room." But now she was beginning to lie. She spoke with passion, but she didn't believe what she said. The poor of Bombay are not beautiful, even with their picturesque costumes in low-caste colors. In complexion, features and physique the poor are distinct from the well-to-do; they are like a race apart, a dwarf race, stunted and slow-witted and made ugly by generations of undernourishment; it will take generations to rehabilitate them. The idea that the poor are beautiful was, with this girl, a borrowed idea. She had converted it into a political attitude, which she was prepared to defend. But it had not sharpened her perception.

New postures in India, attitudes that imply new ways of seeing, often turn out to be a matter of words alone. In their attempts to go beyond the old sentimental abstractions about the poverty of India, and to come to terms with the poor, Indians have to reach outside their civilization, and they are at the mercy then of every kind of imported idea. The intellectual confusion is greater now than in the days of the British, when the world seemed to stand still, the issues were simpler and it was enough for India to assert its Indianness. The poor were background then. Now they press hard, and have to be taken into account.

From the *Indian Express,* October 31, 1975:

Education Minister Prabha Rau has urged scientists and technologists to innovate simpler technology so that it does not become exclusive. Mrs. Rau was speaking as the chief guest at a seminar on science and integrated rural development. . . . She lamented the fact that the youth were not interested in science and technology because "it is not only expensive but the exclusive preserve of a few," and hoped that there would be more "active participation of a larger number of people."

The speech is not easy to understand—the reporter was clearly baffled by what he heard—but it seems to contain a number of different ideas. There is the idea that the poor should also be educated (Indian students, who are assumed in the speech to be middle-class, *are* in fact interested in science); there is the idea that development should affect the greatest number; and there is the new, and unrelated, idea about "intermediate technology," the idea that Indian technology should match Indian resources and take into account the nature of Indian society. The first two ideas are unexceptionable, the third more complex; but, complex or simple, the ideas are so much a matter of words that they have been garbled together— either by the minister or by the reporter—into a kind of political manifesto, an expression of concern with the poor.

The poor are almost fashionable. And this idea of intermediate technology has become an aspect of that fashion. The cult in India centers on the bullock cart. The bullock cart is not to be eliminated; after three thousand or more backward years Indian intermediate technology will now improve the bullock cart. "Do you know," someone said to me in Delhi, "that the investment in bullock carts is equivalent to the total investment in the railways?" I had always had my doubts about bullock carts; but I didn't know until then that they were not cheap, were really quite expensive, more expensive than many second-hand cars in England, and that only richer peasants could afford them. It seemed to me a great waste, the kind of waste that poverty perpetuates. But I was glad I didn't speak, because the man who was giving me these statistics went on: "Now. If we could improve the performance of the bullock cart by ten percent . . ."

What did it mean, improving the performance by 10 percent? Greater speed, bigger loads? Were there bigger loads to carry? These were not the questions to ask, though. Intermediate technology had decided that the bullock cart was to be improved. Metal axles, bearings, rubber tires? But wouldn't that make the carts even more expensive? Wouldn't it take generations, and a lot of money, to introduce those improvements? And, having got so far, mightn't it be better to go just a little further and introduce some harmless little engine? Shouldn't intermediate technology be concentrating on that harmless little engine capable of the short journeys bullock carts usually make?

But no: these were a layman's fantasies: the bullock was, as it were, central to the bullock-cart problem, as the problem had been defined. The difficulty—for science—was the animal's inconvenient shape. The bullock wasn't like the horse: it couldn't be harnessed properly. The bullock carried a yoke on its neck. This had been the practice since the beginning of history, and the time had come for change. This method of yoking was not only inefficient; it also created sores and skin cancer on the bullock's neck and shortened the animal's working life. The bullock-cart enthusiast in Delhi told me that a bullock lasted only three years. But this was the exaggeration of enthusiasm; other people told me that bullocks lasted ten or eleven years. To improve yoking, much research had to be done on the stresses on the bullock as it lifted and pulled. The most modern techniques of monitoring had to be used; and somewhere in the south there was a bullock which, while apparently only going about its peaceful petty business, was as wired up as any cosmonaut.

I was hoping to have a look at this animal when I got to the south and—India being a land of overenthusiastic report—to check with the scientist who had become the bullock-cart king. But the man himself was out of the country, lecturing; he was in demand abroad. Certain subjects, like poverty and intermediate technology, keep the experts busy. They are harassed by international seminars and conferences and foundation fellowships. The rich countries pay; they dictate the guiding ideas, which are the ideas of the rich about the poor, ideas sometimes about what is good for the poor, and sometimes no more than expressions of alarm. They, the rich countries, even manage now to export their romantic doubts about industrial civilization. These are the doubts that attend every kind of great success; and they are romantic because they contain no wish to undo that success or to lose the fruits of that success. But India interprets these doubts in its own debilitating way, and uses them to reconcile itself to its own failure.

Complex imported ideas, forced through the retort of Indian sensibility, often come out cleansed of content, and harmless; they seem so regularly to lead back, through religion and now science, to the past and nullity: to the spinning wheel, the bullock cart. Intermediate technology should mean a leap ahead, a leap beyond accepted solutions, new ways of perceiving coincident needs and resources. In India it has circled back to something very like the old sentimentality about poverty and the old ways, and has stalled with the bullock cart: a fascinating intellectual adventure for the people concerned, but sterile, divorced from reality and usefulness.

And while, in the south, science seeks to improve the bullock cart, at Ahmedabad in Gujarat, at the new, modern and expensively equipped National Institute of Design, they are—on a similar "intermediate" principle and as part of the same cult of the poor—designing or redesigning tools for the peasants. Among the finished products in the glass-walled showroom downstairs was a portable agricultural spraying machine, meant to be carried on the back. The bright yellow plastic casing looked modern enough; but it was hard to know why at Ahmedabad— apart from the anxiety to get the drab thing into bright modern plastic—they had felt the need to redesign this piece of equipment, which on the tea gardens and elsewhere is commonplace and, it might be thought, sufficiently reduced to simplicity. Had something been added? Something had, within the yellow plastic. A heavy motor, which would have crippled the peasant called upon to carry it for any length of time: the peasant who already, in some parts of India, has to judge tools by their weight and, because he has sometimes to carry his plough long distances to his field, prefers a wooden plough to an iron one. My guide acknowledged that the spray was heavy, but gave no further explanation.

The spraying machine, however, was of the modern age. Upstairs, a fourth-year student, clearly one of the stars of the Institute, was designing tools for the ancient world. He had a knife-sharpening machine to show; but in what way it differed from other cumbersome knife-sharpening machines I couldn't tell. His chief interest, though, was in tools for reaping. He disapproved of the sickle for some reason; and he was against the scythe because the cut stalks fell too heavily to the ground.

Scythe and sickle were to be replaced by a long-handled tool which looked like a pair of edging shears: roughly made, no doubt because it was for the peasants and had to be kept rough and simple. When placed on the ground, the thick metal blades made a small V; but only one blade was movable, and this blade the peasant had to kick against the fixed blade and then—by means the designer had not yet worked out—retract for the next cut.

As an invention, this seemed to me some centuries behind the reaping machine of ancient Rome (a bullock-pushed tray with a serrated edge); but the designer, who was a townsman, said he had spent a week in the countryside and the peasants had been interested. I said that the tool required the user to stand; Indians preferred to squat while they did certain jobs. He said the people had to be re-educated.

His alternative design absolutely required standing. This was a pair of reaping shoes. At the front of the left shoe was a narrow cutting blade; on the right side of the right shoe was a longer curved blade. So the peasant, advancing through his ripe corn, would kick with his left foot and cut, while with his right he would describe a wide arc and cut: a harvest dance. Which, I felt, explained the otherwise mysterious presence of a wheelchair in the showroom downstairs, among the design items—the yellow agricultural spray, the boards with the logos for various firms, the teacups unsteady on too stylishly narrow a base. The wheelchair must have been for peasants: the hand-propelled inner wheel of the chair, if my trial was valid, would bark the invalid's knuckles against the outer wheel, and the chair itself, when stopped, would tip the invalid forward. Yes, my guide said neutrally, the chair did do that: the invalid had to remember to sit well back.

Yet the chair was in the window as something to show, something designed; and perhaps it was there for no better reason than that it looked modern and imported, proof that India was going ahead. Going ahead downstairs, going piously backward upstairs: India advancing simultaneously on all fronts, responding to every kind of idea at once. The National Institute of Design is the only one of its kind in India; it is fabulously equipped, competition to enter is fierce and standards should be high. But it is an imported idea, an imported institution, and it has been imported whole, just like that. In India it has been easily divorced from its animating principle, reduced to its equipment and has ended—admittedly after a controversial period: a new administrator had just been sent in—as a finishing school for the unacademic young, a playpen, with artisans called in to do the heavy work, like those dispirited men I saw upstairs squatting on the floor and working on somebody's chairs: India's eternal division of labor, frustrating the proclaimed social purpose of the Institute.

Mimicry within mimicry, imperfectly understood idea

within imperfectly understood idea: the second-year girl student in the printing department, not understanding the typographical exercise she had been set, and playing with type like a child with a typewriter, avoiding, in the name of design, anything like symmetry, clarity or logic; the third-year girl student showing a talentless drawing and saying, in unacknowledged paraphrase of Klee, that she had described "the adventures of a line"; and that fourth-year man playing with tools for the peasants. There are times when the intellectual confusion of India seems complete and it seems impossible to get back to clarifying first principles. Which must have been one of the aims of an institute of design: to make people look afresh at the everyday.

An elementary knowledge of the history of technology would have kept that student—and the teachers who no doubt encouraged him—off the absurdity of his tools; even an elementary knowledge of the Indian countryside, elementary vision. Those tools were designed in an institute where there appeared to have been no idea of the anguish of the Indian countryside: the landless or bonded laborers, the child laborers, the too many cheap hands, the petty chopped-up fields, the nullity of the tasks. The whole project answered a fantasy of the peasant's life: the peasant as the man overburdened by the need to gather in his abundant harvest: romance, an idea of the simplicity of the past and pre-industrial life, which is at the back of so much thinking, political and otherwise, in India, the vision based on no vision.

The bullock cart is to be improved by high science. The caravans will plod idyllically to market, and the peasant, curled up on his honest load, will sleep away the night, a man matching his rhythm to that of nature, a man in partnership with his animals. But that same peasant, awake, will goad his bullock in the immemorial way, by pushing a stick up its anus. It is an unregarded but necessary part of the idyll, one of the obscene sights of the Indian road: the hideous cruelty of pre-industrial life, cruelty constant and casual, and easily extended from beast to man.

The beauty of the simple life, the beauty of the poor: in India the ideas are rolled together and appear one, but the ideas are separate and irreconcilable, because they assert two opposed civilizations.

2

Indians say that their gift is for cultural synthesis. When they say this, they are referring to the pre-British past, to the time of Muslim dominance. And though the idea is too much part of received wisdom, too much a substitute for thought and inquiry, there is proof of that capacity for synthesis in Indian painting. For the two hundred years or so of its vigor, until (very roughly) about 1800, this art is open to every kind of influence, even European. It constantly alters and develops as it shifts from center to center, and is full of local surprises. Its inventiveness—which contemporary scholarship is still uncovering—is truly astonishing.

In the nineteenth century, with the coming of the British, this great tradition died. Painting is only as good as its patrons allow it to be. Indian painting, before the British, was an art of the princely courts, Hindu or Muslim, and reflected the culture of those courts. Now there were new patrons, of more limited interests; and nothing is sadder, in the recent history of Indian culture, than to see Indian painting, in its various schools, declining into East India Company art, tourist art. A new way of looking is imposed, and Indian artists become ordinary as they depict native "types" in as European a manner as their techniques allow, or when, suppressing their own idea of their function as craftsmen, their own feeling for design and organization, they struggle with what must have been for them the meaninglessness of Constable-like "views." A vigorous art becomes imitative, second-rate, insecure (always with certain regional exceptions); it knows it cannot compete; it withers away, and is finally abolished by the camera. It is as though, in a conquered Europe, with all of European art abruptly disregarded, artists were required to paint genre pictures in, say, a Japanese manner. It can be done, but the strain will kill.

India has recovered its traditions of the classical dance, once almost extinct, and its weaving arts. But the painting tradition remains broken; painting cannot simply go back to where it left off; too much has intervened. The Indian past can no longer provide inspiration for the Indian present. In this matter of artistic vision the West is too dominant, and too varied; and India continues imitative and insecure, as a glance at the advertisements and illustrations of any Indian magazine will show. India, without its own living traditions, has lost the ability to incorporate and adapt; what it borrows it seeks to swallow whole. For all its appearance of cultural continuity, for all the liveliness of its arts of dance, music and cinema, India is incomplete: a whole creative side has died. It is the price India has had to pay for its British period. The loss balances the intellectual recruitment during this period, the political self-awareness (unprecedented in Indian history) and the political reorganization.

What is true of Indian painting is also true of Indian architecture. There again a tradition has been broken; too much has intervened; and modernity, or what is considered to be modernity, has now to be swallowed whole. The effect is calamitous. Year by year India's stock of barely usable modern buildings grows. Old ideas about ventilation are out; modern air-conditioners are in; they absolve the architect of the need to design for the difficult climate, and leave him free to copy. Ahmedabad doesn't only have the National Institute of Design; it also, as a go-ahead city, has a modern little airport building. The roof isn't flat or sloping, but wavy; and the roof is low. Hot air can't rise too high; and glass walls, decoratively hung with some reticulated modern fabric, let in the Indian afternoon sun. It is better to stay with the taxi-drivers outside, where the temperature is only about a hundred. Inside, fire is being fought with fire, modernity with modernity; the glass oven hums with an expensive, power-consuming "Gulmarg" air-cooler, around which the respectable and sheltered cluster.

At Jaisalmer in the Rajasthan desert the state govern-ment has just built a tourist guest house of which it is very proud. Little rooms open off a central corridor, and the desert begins just outside the uncanopied windows. But the rooms needn't be stuffy. For ten rupees extra a day you can close the shutters, switch on the electric light, and use the cooler, an enormous factory fan set in the window, which makes the little room roar. Yet Jaisalmer is famous for its old architecture, its palaces and the almost Venetian grandeur of some of its streets. And in the bazaar area there are traditional courtyard houses, in mag-nificent stone versions for the desert: tall, permitting ventilation in the outer rooms, some part of the house always in cool shadow.

But the past is the past: architecture in India is a modern course of study and, as such, another imported skill, part of someone else's tradition. In architecture as in art, without the security of a living tradition, India is disadvantaged. Modernity—or Indianness—is so often only a matter of a façade; within, and increasingly, even in remote places now, is a nightmare of misapplied technology or misunderstood modern design: the rooms built as if for Siberia, always artificially lit, noisy with the power-consuming air-conditioning unit, and uninhabitable without that unit, which leaks down the walls and ruins the fitted carpet: expense upon expense, the waste with which ignorance often burdens poverty.

There was a time when Indians who had been abroad and picked up some simple degree or skill said that they had become displaced and were neither of the East nor West. In this they were absurd and self-dramatizing: they carried India with them, Indian ways of perceiving. Now, with the great migrant rush, little is heard of that displacement. Instead, Indians say that they have become too educated for India. The opposite is usually true: they are not educated enough; they only want to repeat their lessons. The imported skills are rooted in nothing; they are skills separate from principles.

On the train going back to Bombay one rainy evening I heard the complaint from a blank-faced, plump young man. He was too educated for India, he said; and he spoke the worn words without irony or embarrassment. He had done a course in computers in the United States, and (having money) what he wanted to do was to set up a factory to build the American equipment he had learned about. But India wasn't ready for this kind of advanced equipment, and he was thinking he might have to go back permanently to the United States.

I wanted to hear more about his time in the United States. But he had little else to say about that country or—the rainy, smoky industrial outskirts of Bombay, rust, black and green, going past our window—about India. America was as he had expected it to be, he said. He gave no concrete details. And India—even after the United States, and in spite of what could be seen through our window—he assessed only as an entrepreneur might assess it.

He was of a northern merchant caste; he carried caste in his manner. He belonged to old India; nothing had happened to shake him out of that security; he questioned nothing. From the outside world he had snatched no more than a skill in computers, as in less complicated times he might have learned about cloth or grain at home. He said he was too educated for India. But—to give the example given me by the engineer I had got to know in Bombay—he was like the plumber from the slums: a man from a simple background called upon to exercise a high skill, and exercising it blindly. Water is the plumber's business; but water is to him a luxury, something for which his wife has to stand in line every morning; he cannot then understand why it is necessary for a tap to be placed straight, in the center of a tile. So—in spite of his own simple background, in spite of India—the computer man, possessing only his specialized skill, saw his business as the laying down of computers, anywhere.

To match technology to the needs of a poor country calls for the highest skills, the clearest vision. Old India, with all its encouragements to the instinctive, non-intellectual life, limits vision. And the necessary attempt at making imported technology less "exclusive"—to use the confusing and perhaps confused word of the Maharashtra education minister—has ended with the school of the bullock cart, a mixture of mimicry and fantasy. Yet it is something—perhaps a great deal—that India has felt the need to make the attempt.

3

India is old, and India continues. But all the disciplines and skills that India now seeks to exercise are borrowed. Even the ideas Indians have of the achievements of their civilization are essentially the ideas given them by European scholars in the nineteenth century. India by itself could not have rediscovered or assessed its past. Its past was too much with it, was still being lived out in the ritual, the laws, the magic—the complex instinctive life that muffles response and buries even the idea of inquiry. Indian painting now has its scholars in India, but the approach to painting, even among educated people, is still, generally, iconographic, the recognition of deities and themes. A recently dead tradition, an unchanging belief: the creative loss passes unnoticed.

India blindly swallows its past. To understand that past, it has had to borrow alien academic disciplines; and, as with the technology, their foreign origin shows. Much historical research has been done; but European methods of historical inquiry, arising out of one kind of civilization, with its own developing ideas of the human condition, cannot be applied to Indian civilization; they miss too much. Political or dynastic events, economic life, cultural trends: the European approach elucidates little, has the effect of an unsuccessful attempt to equate India with Europe, and makes nonsense of the stops and starts of Indian civilization, the brief flowerings, the long periods of sterility, men forever claimed by the instinctive life, continuity turning to barbarism.

History, with its nationalist shrillness, sociology with its mathematical approach and its tables: these borrowed disciplines remain borrowed. They have as yet given India little idea of itself. India no more possesses Indian history than it possesses its art. People have an idea of the past and can quote approving things from foreign sources (a habit of which all Indians complain and of which all are guilty). But to know India, most people look inward. They consult themselves: in their own past, in the nature of their caste or clan life, their family traditions, they find the idea of India which they know to be true, and according to which they act.

Indian newspapers reflect this limited vision, this absence of inquiry, the absence of what can be called human interest. The precensorship liveliness of the Indian press—of which foreign observers have spoken—was confined to the editorial pages. Elsewhere there were mainly communiqués, handouts, reports of speeches and functions. Indian journalism developed no reporting tradition; it often reported on India as on a foreign country. An unheadlined item from the *Statesman,* September 17, 1975:

Woman Jumps to Death: A woman jumped to death after throwing her two children into a well at Chennaptna, 60 km from Bangalore recently, according to police—PTI.

Recently! But that is all; the police communiqué is enough; no reporter was sent out to get the story. From the *Times of India,* October 4, 1975:

An "eye-surgeon," who had performed 70 eye operations here in February resulting in the loss of eyesight of 20 persons and serious injuries to many others, has been arrested in Muzaffarnagar, the police said there yesterday. The man, apparently an Ayurvedic physician with no knowledge of surgery, had promised patients in Jalgaon that he would perform the operations at concessional rates.

That is all; the story is over; there will be no more tomorrow.

A caste vision: what is remote from me is remote from me. The Indian press has interpreted its function in an Indian way. It has not sought to put India in touch with itself; it doesn't really know how, and it hasn't felt the need. During its free years it watched over nothing; away from the political inferno of its editorial pages it saw few causes for concern. Its India was background, was going on. It was a small-circulation left-wing paper, the *Economic and Political Weekly* of Bombay, that exposed the abuses on the coalfields in the Dhanbad district of Bihar, where workers were terrorized by moneylenders and their gangs. Shortly after the Emergency, the government announced that two or three hundred of the moneylenders had been arrested. That, too, was a simple agency item in the Indian daily press. No paper related it to what had gone before, or seemed to understand its importance; no one went out to investigate the government's claim. Only, some time later, the Calcutta *Statesman* carried an account by a reporter of what it felt like to go down a pit at Dhanbad: a "color" piece, cast in terms of personal adventure, an Indian account, with the miners as background.

Since the Emergency the government—for obvious reasons—has decreed that newspapers should look away from politics and concentrate on social issues. It has required newspapers to go in for "investigative reporting"—the borrowed words are used; and it might be said that the news about India in the Indian press has never been so bad as it is now. Recent numbers of the *Illustrated Weekly of India* (adventurously edited, even before the Emergency) have carried features on bonded labor, child labor and child marriage. The Indian press has at last begun to present India to itself. But it does so under compulsion. It is one of the paradoxes of India under the Emergency that make judgment about the Emergency so difficult: the dangers are obvious, but the results can appear positive. The press has lost its political freedom, but it has extended its interpretative function.

The press (like technology, eventually) can be made to match Indian needs. But what of the law? How can that system, bequeathed to India by another civilization with other values, give India equity and perform the law's constant reassessing, reforming role? From the *Times of India,* October 5, 1975:

The Prime Minister, Mrs. Indira Gandhi, said today that the Indian legal system should assume a "dynamic role" in the process of social transformation, shaking off the "inhibiting legacy of the colonial past." . . . She said: "Law should be an instrument of social justice." Explaining the "dynamic role" of the legal system, Mrs. Gandhi said it should assist in the liberation of the human spirit and of human institutions from the straitjacket of outdated customs. She said the people's respect for law depended on the extent of their conviction that it afforded them real and impartial protection. "Our ancients realized this when they stated that society should uphold dharma so that dharma sustains society," she added.

But how can the imported system assume its dynamic role in India? The difficulty, the contradiction, lies in that very concept of *dharma*. The *dharma* of which Mrs. Gandhi speaks is a complex word: it can mean the faith, pietas, everything which is felt to be right and religious and sanctioned. Law must serve *dharma* or at least not run counter to it; and that seems fair enough. Yet *dharma,* as expressed in the Indian social system, is so shot through with injustice and cruelty, based on such a limited view of man. It can accommodate bonded labor as, once, it accommodated widow-burning. *Dharma* can resist the idea of equity. Law in India can at times appear a forensic game, avoiding collision with the abuses it should be remedying; and it is hard to see how any system of law can do otherwise while the Indian social system holds, and while *dharma* is honored above the simple rights of men.

A. S. R. Chari is a famous Indian criminal lawyer. He has written a book about some of his cases; and in October 1975 *Blitz,* a popular left-wing weekly of Bombay, retold this story from the Chari book. In Maharashtra, in the 1950s, a marriage was arranged between the daughter of a cloth-seller and the son of a lawyer. The lawyer turned up for the wedding ceremony with 150 guests, all to be fed and lodged at the cloth-seller's expense. The cloth-seller objected; the lawyer, angered by the discourtesy and apparent meanness, threw two thousand rupees in notes at the feet of the cloth-seller in a gesture of insult. Yet the marriage went ahead: the lawyer's son married the cloth-seller's daughter. Only, the lawyer forbade his son to have anything more to do with his wife's family, and forbade his daughter-in-law to visit her parents. The girl suffered. ("She seemed to have been a highly strung girl," Chari writes.) She suffered especially when she was not allowed to visit her sister in hospital. Her husband was firm when she asked his permission. He said: "You know the position. I cannot allow this. Do not be too unhappy over it." Waking up that night, the young man found his wife dead beside him.

Cyanide was detected in the viscera of the dead girl; and the young man was charged with her murder. The prosecution argued that she could not, by herself, have obtained the cyanide in Bombay; it must have been administered by her husband, who, as a photographer, had chemicals of various kinds in his laboratory. But the police hadn't found potassium or sodium cyanide in the laboratory; they had only found potassium ferricyanide, not a poison. This gave Chari—arguing the young man's appeal against conviction for murder—his clue. "Potassium ferricyanide, though not ordinarily a poison, would act as a poison when taken by a person who had hyper-acidity—that is, a person who secreted too much hydro-chloric acid in the stomach." So the girl had committed suicide. Her husband was acquitted.

Justice was done. But the injustice to the dead girl was hardly commented on. The Supreme Court, hearing the appeal, spoke of "false ideas of family prestige"; but in Chari's legalistic account, as rendered in *Blitz,* full of technicalities about the admissibility of evidence, the punishment of the cloth-seller by the suicide of his daughter is made to appear just one of those things. "Oh yes," one of the appeal judges said, "you have to make arrangements so thoroughly that you satisfy every demand made by any one of the bridegroom's party." And in this acknowledgment of the traditional demands of family honor the tragedy of the girl is lost: writing letters to the family she is not allowed to see ("God's will be done"), so quickly accepting that her young life is spoiled and has to be ended.

The law avoids the collision with *dharma*. Yet it is this *dharma* that the law must grapple with if the law is to have a "dynamic role." That is the difficulty: to cope with the new pressures, India has in some ways to undermine itself, to lose its old security. Borrowed institutions can no longer function simply as borrowed institutions, a tribute to modernity. Indians say that their gift is for synthesis. It might be said, rather, that for too long, as a conquered people, they have been intellectually parasitic on other civilizations. To survive in subjection, they have preserved their sanctuary of the instinctive, uncreative life, converting that into a religious ideal; at a more worldly level, they have depended on others for the ideas and institutions that make a country work. The Emergency—coming so soon after Independence—dramatizes India's creative incapacity, its intellectual depletion, its defenselessness, the inadequacy of every Indian's idea of India.

A NEW KING FOR THE CONGO:
MOBUTU AND THE NIHILISM
OF AFRICA

January–March 1975

The Congo, which used to be a Belgian colony, is now an African kingdom and is called Zaire. It appears to be a nonsense name, a sixteenth-century Portuguese corruption, some Zairois will tell you, of a local word for "river." So it is as if Taiwan, reasserting its Chinese identity, were again to give itself the Portuguese name Formosa. The Congo River is now called the Zaire, as is the local currency, which is almost worthless.

The man who has made himself king of this land of the three Zs—*pays, fleuve, monnaie*—used to be called Joseph Mobutu. His father was a cook. But Joseph Mobutu was educated; he was at some time, in the Belgian days, a journalist. In 1960, when the country became independent, Mobutu was thirty, a sergeant in the local Force Publique. The Force Publique became the Congolese National

Army. Mobutu became the colonel and commander, and through the mutinies, rebellions and secessions of the years after independence he retained the loyalty of one paratroop brigade. In 1965, as General Mobutu, he seized power; and as he has imposed order on the army and the country so his style has changed, and become more African. He has abandoned the name of Joseph and is now known as Mobutu Sese Seko Kuku Ngbendu Wa Za Banga.

As General Mobutu he used to be photographed in army uniform. Now, as Mobutu Sese Seko, he wears what he has made, by his example, the Zairois court costume. It is a stylish version of the standard two-piece suit. The jacket has high, wide lapels and is buttoned all the way down; the sleeves can be long or short. A boldly patterned cravat replaces the tie, which has more or less been outlawed; and a breast-pocket handkerchief matches the cravat. On less formal occasions—when he goes among the people—Mobutu wears flowered shirts. Always, in public, he wears a leopard-skin cap and carries an elaborately carved stick.

These—the cap and the stick—are the emblems of his African chieftaincy. Only the chief can kill the leopard. The stick is carved with symbolic figures: two birds, what looks like a snake, a human figure with a distended belly. No Zairois I met could explain the symbolism. One teacher pretended not to know what was carved, and said, "We would all like to have sticks like that." In some local carving, though, the belly of the human figure is distended because it contains the fetish. The stick is accepted by Zairois as the stick of the chief. While the chief holds the stick off the ground the people around him can speak; when the chief sets his stick on the ground the people fall silent and the chief gives his decision.

Explaining the constitution and the president's almost unlimited powers, *Profils du Zaire,* the new official handbook (of variable price: four zaires, eight dollars, the pavement seller's "first" price, two zaires his "last" price), *Profils du Zaire* quotes Montesquieu on the functions of the state. *Elima,* the official daily, has another, African view of government. "In Zaire we have inherited from our ancestors a profound respect for the liberties of others. This is why our ancestors were so given to conciliation, people accustomed to the palaver [*la palabre*], accustomed, that is, to discussions that established each man in his rights."

So Montesquieu and the ancestors are made to meet. And ancestral ways turn out to be advanced. It is only a matter of finding the right words. The palaver is, after all, a "dialogue"; chief's rule is government by dialogue. But when the chief speaks, when the chief sets his carved stick on the ground, the modern dialogue stops; and Africa of the ancestors takes over. The chief's words, as *Elima* (having it all ways) has sometimes to remind "anti-revolutionary" elements, cannot be questioned.

It is said that the last five words of Mobutu's African name are a reference to the sexual virility which the African chief must possess: he is the cock that leaves no hen alone. But the words may only be symbolic. Because, as chief, Mobutu is "married" to his people—"The Marriage of Sese [Mobutu]" is a "revolutionary" song—and, as in the good old days of the ancestors, *comme au bon vieux temps de nos ancêtres,* the chief always holds fast to his people. This marriage of the chief can be explained in another, more legalistic way: the chief has a "contract" with his people. He fulfills his contract through the apparatus of a modern state, but the ministers and commissioners are only the chief's "collaborators," "the umbilical cord between the power and the people."

The chief, the lord wedded to his people, *le pouvoir:* the attributes begin to multiply. Mobutu is also the Guide of the Authentic Zairois Revolution, the Father of the Nation, the President-Founder of the Mouvement Populaire de la Révolution, the country's only political party. So that, in nomenclature as in the stylish national dress he has devised, he combines old Africa with what is progressive and new. Just as a Guy Dormeuil suit (160 zaires in the Kinshasa shops, 320 dollars) can, with cravat and matching handkerchief, become an authentic Zairois national costume, so a number of imported glamorous ideas bolster Mobutu's African chieftaincy.

He is citizen, chief, king, revolutionary; he is an African

freedom fighter; he is supported by the spirits of the ancestors; like Mao, he has published a book of thoughts (Mobutu's book is green). He has occupied every ideological position and the basis of his kingship cannot be questioned. He rules; he is grand; and, like a medieval king, he is at once loved and feared. He controls the armed forces; they are his creation; in Kinshasa he still sleeps in an army camp. Like Leopold II of the Belgians, in the time of the Congo Free State—much of whose despotic legislation (ownership of the mines in 1888, all vacant lands in 1890, the fruits of the earth in 1891) has passed down through the Belgian colonial administration to the present regime, and is now presented as a kind of ancestral African socialism—like Leopold II, Mobutu owns Zaire.

Muhammad Ali fought George Foreman in Kinshasa last November. Ali won; but the victor, in Zaire, was Mobutu. A big hoarding outside the stadium still says, in English below the French: "A fight between two Blacks [*deux noirs*], in a Black Nation [*un pays de Nègres*] organized by Blacks and seen by the whole [world] that is a victory of Mobutism." And whatever pleasure people had taken in that event, and the publicity, had been dissipated by mid-January, when I arrived. I had chosen a bad time. Mobutu, chieflike, had sprung another of his surprises. A fortnight before, after a two-day palaver with his collaborators, Mobutu had decided on a "radicalization of the revolution." And everybody was nervous.

In November 1973 Mobutu had nationalized all businesses and plantations belonging to foreigners—mainly Greeks, Portuguese and Indians—and had given them to Zairois. Now, a year later, he had decided to take back these enterprises, many of them pillaged and bankrupt, and entrust them to the state. What, or who, was the state? No one quite knew. New people, more loyal people? Mobutu, speaking the pure language of revolution, seemed to threaten everybody. The three hundred Belgian families who had ruled the Congo, he said, had been replaced by three hundred Zairois families; the country had imported more Mercedes-Benz motorcars than tractors; one third of the country's foreign earnings went to import food that could be produced at home.

Against this new Zairois bourgeoisie—which he had himself created—the chief now declared war. "I offer them a clear choice: those among them who love the people should give everything to the state and follow me." In his new mood the chief threatened other measures. He threatened to close down the cinemas and the nightclubs; he threatened to ban drinking in public places before six.

Through the Belgian-designed *cité indigène* of Kinshasa, in the wide, unpaved streets, full of pits and corrugations between mounds of rubbish sometimes as high as the little houses in Mediterranean colors, in the green shade of flamboyant, mango and frangipani, schoolchildren marched in support of their chief. Every day *Elima* carried reports of *marches de soutien* in other places. And the alarm was great, among the foreigners who had been plundered of their businesses and had remained behind, hoping for some compensation or waiting for Canadian visas, and among the gold-decked Zairois in national costume. Stern men, these Zairois, nervous of the visitor, easily affronted, anxious only to make it known that they were loyal, and outdone by no one in their "authenticity," their authentic Africanness.

But it is in the nature of a powerful chief that he should be unpredictable. The chief threatens; the people are cowed; the chief relents; the people praise his magnanimity. The days passed; daytime and even morning drinking didn't stop; many Africans continued to spend their days in that red-eyed vacancy that at first so mystifies the visitor. The nightclubs and cinemas didn't close; the prostitutes continued to be busy around the Memling Hotel. So that it seemed that in this matter of public morals, at least, the chief had relented. The ordinary people had been spared.

But the nervousness higher up was justified. Within days the axe fell on many of the chief's "collaborators." There was a shake-up; the circle of power around the chief was made smaller; and Zairois who had ruled in Kinshasa were abruptly dismissed, packed off to unfamiliar parts of the bush to spread the word of the revolution. *Elima* sped them on their way:

> The political commissioner will no longer be what he was before the system was modified. That is to say, a citizen floating above the day-to-day realities of the people, driving about the streets and avenues of Kinshasa in a Mercedes and knowing nothing of the life of the peasant of Dumi. The political commissioners will live with the people. They will be in the fields, not as masters but as peasants. They will work with the workers, they will share their joys and sorrows. They will in this way better understand the aspirations of the people and will truly become again children of the people.

Words of terror. Because this was the great fear of so many of the men who had come by riches so easily, by simple official plunder, the new men of the new state who, in the name of Africanization and the dignity of Africa, were so often doing jobs for which they were not qualified and often were drawing salaries for jobs they were not doing at all. This, for all their talk of authenticity and the ways of the ancestors, was their fear: to be returned from the sweet corruptions of Kinshasa to the older corruption of the bush, to be returned to Africa.

And the bush is close. It begins just outside the city and goes on forever. The airplane that goes from Kinshasa to Kisangani flies over eight hundred miles of what still looks like virgin forest.

Consider the recent journey of the subregional commissioner of the Equator Region to the settlement of Bomongo. Bomongo lies on the Giri River and is just about one hundred miles north of the big town of Mbandaka, formerly Coquilhatville, the old "Equator station," set down more or less on the line of the Equator, halfway on the Congo or Zaire River between Kinshasa and the Stanley Falls. From Mbandaka a steamer took the commissioner's party up the main river to Lubengo; and there they transferred to a dugout for the twenty-mile passage through the Lubengo "canal" to the Giri River. But the canal for much of its length was only six feet wide, full of snags, and sometimes only twelve inches deep. The outboard motor had to be taken up; paddles had to be used. And there were the mosquitoes:

> At the very entrance to the canal [according to the official report in *Elima*], thousands of mosquitoes cover you from head to ankles, compelling you to move about all the time. . . . After a whole night of insomnia on the Lubengo canal, or rather the "calvary" of Lubengo, where we had

very often to get out in the water and make a superhuman effort to help the paddlers free the pirogue from mud or wood snags, we got to the end of the canal at nine in the morning (we had entered it at 9:30 the previous evening), and so at last we arrived at Bomongo at 12:30, in a state that would have softened the hardest hearts. If we have spoken at some length about the Lubengo canal, it isn't because we want to discourage people from visiting Bomongo by the canal route, but rather to stress one of the main reasons why this place is isolated and seldom visited.

Ignoring his fatigue, *bravant sa fatigue,* the commissioner set to work. He spoke to various groups about the integration of the party and the administration, the need for punctuality, professional thoroughness and revolutionary fervor. The next morning he visited an oil factory in Ebeka district that had been abandoned in 1971 and was now being set going again with the help of a foreign adviser. In the afternoon he spoke out against alcoholism and urged people to produce more. The next day he visited a coffee plantation that had been nationalized in 1973 (the plantations in Zaire were run mainly by Greeks) and given to a Zairois. This particular *attribution* hadn't worked well: the laborers hadn't been paid for the last five months. The laborers complained and the commissioner listened; but what the commissioner did or said wasn't recorded. Everywhere the commissioner went he urged the people, for the sake of their own liberty and well-being, to follow the principles of Mobutism to the letter; everywhere he urged vigilance. Then, leaving Lubengo, Bomongo and Ebeka to the mosquitoes, the commissioner returned to his headquarters. And *Elima* considered the fifteen-day journey heroic enough to give it half a page.

Yet Bomongo, so cut off, is only twenty miles away from the main Congo or Zaire. The roads of the country have decayed; the domestic services of Air Zaire are unreliable; the river remains, in 1975, the great highway of the country. And for nearly a hundred years the river has known steamer traffic. Joseph Conrad, not yet a novelist, going up the river in the wood-burning *Roi des Belges* in 1890, doing eight miles in three hours, halting every night for the cannibal woodcutters to sleep on the river-bank, might have thought he was penetrating to the untouched heart of darkness. But Norman Sherry, the Conrad scholar, has gone among the records and in *Conrad's Western World* has shown that even at the time of Conrad's journey there would have been eleven steamers on the upper river.

The steamers have continued, the Belgian *Otraco* being succeeded by the Zairois *Onatra*. The waterway has been charted: white marker signs are nailed to trees on the banks, the river is regularly cleared of snags. The upstream journey that took one month in Conrad's time now takes seven days; the downstream journey that took a fortnight is now done in five days. The stations have become towns, but they remain what they were: trading outposts. And, in 1975, the journey—one thousand miles between green, flat, almost unchanging country—is still like a journey through nothingness. So little has the vast country been touched: so complete, simple and repetitive still appears the African life through which the traveler swiftly passes.

When the steamer was Belgian, Africans needed a *carte de mérite civique* to travel first class, and third-class African passengers were towed on barges some way behind the steamer. Now the two-tiered third-class barges, rusting, battered, needing paint, full of a busy backyard life, tethered goats and crated chickens packed tight among the passengers, are lashed to the bow of the steamer; and first-class passengers sleep and eat outside their cabin doors in a high, warm smell of smoked fish and smoked monkey.

The *cabine de luxe,* twice as expensive as first class, is used by the sweating *garçon* as a storeroom for his brooms and buckets and rags and as a hiding place for the food, *foo-foo,* he is always on the lookout for: securing half a pound of sugar, for instance, by pouring it into a pot of river-brewed tea, and secreting the tea in the wardrobe until nightfall, when he scratches and bangs and scratches at the door until he is admitted.

The curtains of the *cabine* hang ringless and collapsed.

"C'est pas bon," the *garçon* says. Many lightbulbs are missing; they will now never be replaced; but the empty light brackets on the walls can be used to hang things on. In the bathroom the diseased river water looks unfiltered; the stained and leaking washbasin has been pulled out from the wall; the chrome-plated towel rails are forever empty, their function forgotten; and the holes in the floor are mended, like the holes in a dugout, with what looks like mud. The lavatory cistern ceaselessly flushes. *"C'est pas bon,"* the *garçon* says, as of an irremediable fact of life; and he will not say even this when, on an overcast afternoon, in a temperature of a hundred degrees, the windows of the *cabine de luxe* sealed, the air-conditioning unit fails.

The bar is naked except for three bottles of spirits. Beer is *terminé,* always, though the steamer is full of dazed Africans and the man known as the maître d'hôtel is drunk from early morning. There is beer, of course; but every little service requires a "sweetener." The steamer is an African steamer and is run on African lines. It has been adapted to African needs. It carries passengers, too many passengers for the two lifeboats displayed on the first-class deck; but it is more than a passenger steamer. It is a traveling market; it is, still, all that many of the people who live along the river know of the outside world.

The steamer, traveling downstream from Kisangani, formerly Stanleyville, to Kinshasa, stops only at Bumbe, Lisala and Mbandaka. But it serves the bush all the way down. The bush begins just outside Kisangani. The town ends—the decayed Hôtel des Chutes, the customs shed, the three or four rusting iron barges moored together, the Roman Catholic cathedral, then a large ruin, a few river-side villas—and the green begins: bamboo, thick grass spilling over the riverbanks, the earth showing red, green and red reflected in the smooth water, the sky, as so often here, dark with storm, lit up and trembling as with distant gunfire, the light silver. The wind and rain come; the green bank fades; the water wrinkles, the reflections go, the water shows muddy. Jungle seems to be promised. But the bush never grows high, never becomes forest.

Soon the settlements appear: the low thatched huts in scraped brown yards, thatch and walls the color of the earth, the earth scraped bare for fear of snakes and soldier ants. Boys swim out to the steamer, their twice-weekly excitement; and regularly, to shouts, the trading dugouts come, are skillfully poled in alongside the moving steamer, moored, and taken miles downstream while the goods are unloaded, products of the bush: wicker chairs, mortars carved out of tree trunks, great enamel basins of pineap-ples. Because of the wars, or for some other reason, there are few men here, and the paddlers and traders are all women, or young girls.

When the traders have sold, they buy. In the forward part of the steamer, beyond the second-class W.C.s, water always running off their steel floors, and in the narrow walk beside the cabins, among the defecating babies, the cooking and the washing and the vacant girls being intently deloused, in a damp smell of salted fish and excrement and oil and rust, and to the sound of gramophone records, there are stalls: razor blades, batteries, pills and capsules, soap, hypodermic syringes, cigarettes, pencils, copybooks, lengths of cloth. These are the products of the outside world that are needed; these are the goods for which such exertions are made. Their business over, the dugouts cast off, to paddle lightless upstream miles in the dark.

There can be accidents (a passenger dugout joining the moving steamer was to be overturned on this journey, and some students returning from the bush to Kinshasa were to be lost); and at night the steamer's searchlights constantly sweep the banks. Moths show white in the light; and on the water the Congo hyacinth shows white: a water plant that appeared on the upper Congo in 1956 and has since spread all the way down, treacherously beautiful, with thick lilylike green leaves and a pale-lilac flower like a wilder hyacinth. It seeds itself rapidly; it can form floating islands that attract other vegetation; it can foul the propellers of the steamer. If the steamers do not fail, if there are no more wars, it is the Congo hyacinth that may yet imprison the river people in the immemorial ways of the bush.

In the morning there are new dugouts, fresh merchandise: basins of slugs in moist black earth, fresh fish and monkeys, monkeys ready-smoked, *boucané,* charred little hulks, or freshly killed, gray or red monkeys, the tips of their tails slit, the slit skin of the tail tied round the neck, the monkeys bundled up and lifted in this way from the dugouts, by the tails, holdalls, portmanteaux, of dead monkeys. The excitement is great. Monkey is an African delicacy, and a monkey that fetches six zaires, twelve dollars, in Kinshasa can be bought on the river for three zaires.

On the throbbing steel deck the monkeys can appear to be alive and breathing. The wind ruffles their fur; the faces of the red monkeys, falling this way and that, suggest deep contented sleep; their forepaws are loosely closed, sometimes stretched out before them. At the stern of the steamer, on the lower deck, a wood fire is lit and the cooking starts: the dead monkey held face down over the fire, the fur burned off. In the bow, among the goats and hens, there is a wet baby monkey, tightly tethered, somebody's pet or somebody's supper (and in the lifeboat there will appear the next day, as a kind of African joke, a monkey's skull, picked clean and white).

So day after day, through the halts at Bumbe, Lisala and Mbandaka—the two-storied Belgian colonial buildings, the ochre concrete walls, the white arches, the green or red corrugated-iron roofs—the steamer market goes on. On the riverbanks bamboo gives way to palms, their lower brown fronds brushing the yellow water. But there is no true forest. The tall trees are dead, and their trunks and bare branches stick out white above the low green bush. The lower vegetation is at times tattered, and sometimes opens out into grassy savanna land, blasted-looking and ghostly in the afternoon heat mist.

The river widens; islands appear; but there is no solitude in this heart of Africa. Always there are the little brown settlements in scraped brown yards, the little plantings of maize or banana or sugarcane about huts, the trading dugouts arriving beside the steamer to shouts. In the heat mist the sun, an hour before sunset, can appear round and orange, reflected in an orange band in the water muddy with laterite, the orange reflection broken only by the ripples from the bows of the steamer and the barges. Sometimes at sunset the water will turn violet below a violet sky.

But it is a peopled wilderness. The land of this river basin is land used in the African way. It is burned, cultivated, abandoned. It looks desolate, but its riches and fruits are known; it is a wilderness, but one of monkeys. Bush and blasted trees disappear only towards Kinshasa. It is only after nine hundred miles that earth and laterite give way to igneous rocks, and the land, becoming hilly, with sharp indentations, grows smooth and bare, dark with vegetation only in its hollows.

Plant today, reap tomorrow: this is what they say in Kisangani. But this vast green land, which can feed the continent, barely feeds itself. In Kinshasa the meat and even the vegetables have to be imported from other countries. Eggs and orange juice come from South Africa, in spite of hot official words; and powdered milk and bottled milk come from Europe. The bush is a way of life; and where the bush is so overwhelming, organized agriculture is an illogicality.

The Belgians, in the last twenty years of their rule, tried to develop African agriculture, and failed. A girl on the steamer, a teacher, remembered the irrational attempt, and the floggings. Agriculture had to be "industrialized," a writer said one day in *Elima,* but not in the way "the old colonialists and their disciples have preached." The Belgians failed because they were too theoretical, too removed from the peasants, whom they considered "ignorant" and "irrational." In Zaire, as in China, according to this writer, a sound agriculture could only be based on traditional methods. Machines were not necessary. They were not always suited to the soil; tractors, for instance, often made the soil infertile.

Two days later there was another article in *Elima.* It was no secret, the writer said, that the agriculturists of the country cultivated only small areas and that their production was "minimal." Modern machines had to be used: North Korean experts were coming to show the people how. And there was a large photograph of a tractor, a promise of the future.

About agriculture, as about so many things, as about

the principles of government itself, there is confusion. Everyone feels the great bush at his back. And the bush remains the bush, with its own logical life. Away from the mining areas and the decaying towns the land is as the Belgians found it and as they have left it.

Aperire terram gentibus: "To Open the Land to the Nations": this is the motto, in raised granite, that survives over the defaced monument at Kinshasa railway station. The railway from the Atlantic, the steamer beyond the rapids at Kinshasa: this was how the Congo was opened up, and the monument was erected in 1948 to mark the first fifty years of the railway.

But now the railway is used mainly for goods. Few visitors arrive at the little suburban-style station, still marked "Kinshasa Est," and step out into the imperial glory of the two-lane boulevard that runs south of the river, just behind the docks. In the roundabout outside the station, the statue of King Albert I, uniformed, with sun helmet and sword (according to old postcards, which continue to be sold), has been taken down; the bronze plaques beside the plinth have been broken away, except for an upper fringe of what looks like banana leaves; the floodlamps have been smashed, the wiring apparatus pulled out and rusted; and all that remains of the monument are two tall brick pillars, like the pillars at the end of some abandoned Congolese Appian Way.

In the station hall the timetable frames swivel empty and glassless on the metal pole. But in the station yard, past the open, unguarded doors, there is a true relic: an 1893 locomotive, the first used on the Congo railway. It stands on a bed of fresh gravel, amid croton plants and beside two traveler's-trees. It is small, built for a narrow gauge, and looks quaint, with its low, slender boiler, tall funnel and its open cab; but it still appears whole. It is stamped *No. 1* and in an oval cartouche carries one of the great names of the Belgian nineteenth-century industrial expansion: *Société Anonyme John Cockerill—Seraing.*

Not many people in Kinshasa know about this locomotive; and perhaps it has survived because, like so many things of the Belgian past, it is now junk. Like the half-collapsed fork-lift truck on the platform of one of the goods sheds; like the other fork-lift truck in the yard, more thoroughly pillaged, and seemingly decomposed about its rusted forks, which lie in the dust like metal tusks. Like the one-wheel lawn mower in the park outside, which is now a piece of wasteland, overgrown where it has not been scuffed to dust. The lawn mower is in the possession of a little boy, and he, noticing the stranger's interest, rights his machine and skillfully runs it on its one wheel through the dust, making the rusted blades whirr.

The visitor nowadays arrives at the airport of Ndjili, some miles to the east of the city. Zaire is not yet a land for the casual traveler—the harassments, official and unofficial, are too many—and the visitor is usually either a businessman or, if he is black, a delegate (in national costume) to one of the many conferences that Zaire now hosts. From the airport one road leads to the city and the Intercontinental Hotel, past great green-and-yellow boards with Mobutu's sayings in French and English, past the river (the slums of the *cité indigène* well to the south), past the Belgian-built villas in green gardens. A quiet six-lane highway runs twenty or thirty miles in the other direction, to the "presidential domain" of Nsele.

Here, in what looks like a resort development, flashy but with hints of perishability, distinguished visitors stay or confer, and good members of the party are admitted to a taste of luxury. Muhammad Ali trained here last year; in January this year some North Korean acrobats and United Nations people were staying. There are air-conditioned bungalows, vast meeting halls, extravagant lounges, a swimming pool. There is also a model farm run by the Chinese. Nsele is in the style of the new presidency: one of the many grandiloquent official buildings, chief's compounds, that have been set up in the derelict capital in recent years, at once an assertion of the power of the chief and of the primacy of Africa. In the new palace for visiting heads of state the baths are gold-plated: my informant was someone from another African country, who had stayed there.

So the Belgian past recedes and is made to look as shabby as its defaced monuments. *Elima* gives half a page to the fifteen-day journey of the Equator subcommissioner to Bomongo; but Stanley, who pioneered the Congo route, who built the road from the port of Matadi to Kinshasa, has been dethroned. In the museum a great iron wheel from one of the wagons used on that road is preserved by the Belgian curator (and what labor that wheel speaks of); but Mount Stanley is now Mont Ngaliema, a presidential park; and the statue of Stanley that overlooked the rapids has been replaced by the statue of a tall anonymous tribesman with a spear. At the Hôtel des Chutes in Kisangani the town's old name of Stanleyville survives on some pieces of crockery. The broken coffee cups are now used for sugar and powdered milk; when they go the name will have vanished.

The Belgian past is being scrubbed out as the Arab past has been scrubbed out. The Arabs were the Belgians' rivals in the eastern Congo; an Arab was once governor of the Stanley Falls station. But who now associates the Congo with a nineteenth-century Arab empire? A Batetela boy remembered that his ancestors were slave-catchers for the Arabs; they changed sides when the Belgians came and offered them places in their army. But that was long ago. The boy is now a student of psychology, on the lookout, like so many young Zairois, for some foreign scholarship; and the boy's girlfriend, of another tribe, people in the past considered enslavable, laughed at this story of slave trading.

The bush grows fast over what were once great events or great disturbances. Bush has buried the towns the Arabs planned, the orchards they planted, as recently, during the post-independence troubles, bush buried the fashionable eastern suburbs of Stanleyville, near the Tshopo falls. The Belgian villas were abandoned; the Africans came first to squat and then to pillage, picking the villas clean of metal, wire, timber, bathtubs and lavatory bowls (both useful for soaking manioc in), leaving only ground-floor shells of brick and masonry. In 1975 some of the ruins still stand, and they look very old, like a tropical, overgrown Pompeii, cleared of its artifacts, with only the ruins of the Château de Venise nightclub giving a clue to the cultural life of the vanished settlement.

And it is surprising how, already, so little of Belgium remains in the minds of people. A man of forty—he had spent some years in the United States—told me that his father, who was born in 1900, remembered the Belgian rubber levy and the cutting off of hands. A woman said that her grandfather had brought white priests to the village to protect the villagers against harsh officials. But, ironically, the people who told these stories both might have been described as *évolués.* Most people under thirty,

breaking out of the bush into teaching jobs and adminis-
trative jobs in Kinshasa, said they had heard nothing about
the Belgians from their parents or grandparents.

One man, a university teacher, said, "The Belgians gave
us a state. Before the Belgians came we had no state."
Another man said he had heard from his grandfather only
about the origins of the Bantu people: they wandered
south from Lake Chad, crossed the river into an "empty"
country, inhabited only by pygmies, "a primitive people,"
whom they drove away into the deep forest. For most the
past is a blank; and history begins with their own memo-
ries. Most record a village childhood, a school, and then—
the shock of independence. To a man from Bandundu,
the son of a "farmer," and the first of his village to be educated, the new world came suddenly in 1960 with the
arrival in his village of soldiers of the disintegrating Congolese army. "I saw soldiers for the first time then, and I
was very frightened. They had no officers. They treated
the women badly and killed some men. The soldiers were
looking for white people."

In the colonial days, a headmaster told me, the school
histories of the Congo began with the late-fifteenth-
century Portuguese navigators, and then jumped to the
nineteenth century, to the missionaries and the Arabs and
the Belgians. African history, as it is now written, restores
Africans to Africa, but it is no less opaque: a roll call of
tribes, a mention of great kingdoms. So it is in *Introduction*

à l'Histoire de l'Afrique Noire, published in Zaire last year. So it is in the official *Profils du Zaire,* which—ignoring Portuguese, missionaries and Arabs—jumps from the brief mention of mostly undated African kingdoms to the establishment of the Congo Free State. The tone is cool and legalistic. King Leopold II's absolute powers are spoken of in just the same way as the powers of older African kings. Passion enters the story only with the events of independence.

The past has vanished. Facts in a book cannot by themselves give people a sense of history. Where so little has changed, where bush and river are so overwhelming, another past is accessible, better answering African bewilderment and African religious beliefs: the past as *le bon vieux temps de nos ancêtres.*

In the presidential park at Mont Ngaliema, formerly Mount Stanley, where the guards wear decorative uniforms, and the gates are decorated with bronze plaques— the bad art of modern Africa: art that no longer serves a religious or magical purpose, attempts an alien representationalism and becomes mannered and meaningless, suggesting a double mimicry: African art imitating itself, imitating African-inspired Western art—on Mont Ngaliema there are some colonial graves of the 1890s.

They have been gathered together in neat terraces and

are screened by cypress and flamboyant. There, above the rapids—the brown river breaking white on the rocks but oddly static in appearance, the white crests never moving: an eternal level sound of water—the pioneers grandly lie. The simple professions recur: *commis, agent commercial, chaudronnier* [boilermaker], *capitaine de steamboat, prêtre, s/officier de la Force Publique.* Only Madame Bernard is *sans profession.* Not all were Belgians; some were Norwegians; one missionary was English.

In one kind of imperialist writing these people are heroic. Joseph Conrad, in his passage through the Congo in 1890, just before those burials began on Mont Ngaliema, saw otherwise. He saw people who were too simple for an outpost of progress, people who were part of the crowd at home, and dependent on that crowd, their strength in Africa, like the strength of the Romans in Britain, "an accident arising from the weakness of others," their "conquest of the earth" unredeemed by an idea, "not a sentimental pretence but an idea; and an unselfish belief in the idea."

"In a hundred years," Conrad makes one of these simple people say in "An Outpost of Progress" (1897), "there will perhaps be a town here. Quays, and warehouses, and barracks, and—and—billiard-rooms. Civilization, my boy, and virtue—and all." That civilization, so accurately defined, came; and then, like the villas at Stanleyville and the Château de Venise nightclub, vanished. "Acquisitions, clothes, pretty rags—rags that would fly off at the first good shake": this is from the narrator of *Heart of Darkness* (1902). "No; you want a deliberate belief."

The people who come now—after the general flight—are like the people who came then. They offer goods, deals, technical skills, the same perishable civilization; they bring nothing else. They are not pioneers; they know they cannot stay. They fill the nightclubs (now with African names); they keep the prostitutes (now in African dress; foreign dress is outlawed for African women) busy around the Memling Hotel. So, encircled by Africa, now dangerous again, with threats of expulsion and confiscation, outpost civilization continues: at dinnertime in the Café de la Paix the two old men parade the young prostitutes they have picked up, girls of fourteen or fifteen. Old men: their last chance to feed on such young blood: Kinshasa may close down tomorrow.

"Everyone is here only for the money." The cynicism has never been secret; it is now reinforced by anxiety. With this cynicism, in independent Zaire, the African can appear to be in complicity. He, too, wants "acquisitions, clothes, pretty rags": the Mercedes, the fatter prostitutes, the sharp suit with matching handkerchief and cravat, the gold-rimmed glasses, the gold pen-and-pencil set, the big gold wristwatch on one hand and the gold bracelet on the other, the big belly that in a land of puny men speaks of wealth. But with this complicity and imitation there is something else: a resentment of the people imitated, the people now known as *nostalgiques.*

Simon's company, a big one, has been nationalized, and Simon is now the manager. (Expatriates continue to do the work, but this is only practical, and Simon doesn't mind.) Why then does Simon, who has a background of bush, who is so young and successful, remember his former manager as a *nostalgique?* Well, one day the manager was looking through the pay sheets and he said, "Simon isn't paying enough tax."

People like Simon (he has an official African name) are not easy to know—even Belgians who speak African languages say that. Simon only answers questions; he is incapable of generating anything like a conversation; because of his dignity, his new sense of the self, the world has closed up for him again; and he appears to be hiding. But his resentment of the former manager must have a deeper cause than the one he has given. And gradually it becomes apparent, from other replies he gives, from his belief in "authenticity," from his dislike of foreign attitudes to African art (to him a living thing: he considers the Kinshasa museum an absurdity), from the secretive African arrangements of his domestic life (to which he returns in his motorcar), it gradually becomes apparent that Simon is adrift and nervous in this unreal world of imitation.

It is with people like Simon, educated, moneymaking, that the visitor feels himself in the presence of vulnerability, dumbness, danger. Because their resentments, which appear to contradict their ambitions, and which they can never satisfactorily explain, can at any time be converted into a wish to wipe out and undo, an African nihilism, the rage of primitive men coming to themselves and finding that they have been fooled and affronted.

A rebellion like this occurred after independence. It was led by Pierre Mulele, a former minister of education, who, after a long march through the country, camped at Stanleyville and established a reign of terror. Everyone who could read and write had been taken out to the little park and shot; everyone who wore a tie had been shot. These were the stories about Mulele that were circulating in neighboring Uganda in 1966, nearly two years after the rebellion had been put down (Uganda itself about to crumble, its nihilistic leader already apparent: Amin, the commander of the petty army that had destroyed the Kabaka's power). Nine thousand people are said to have died in Mulele's rebellion. What did Mulele want? What was the purpose of the killings? The forty-year-old African who had spent some time in the United States laughed and said, "Nobody knows. He was against *everything*. He wanted to start again from the beginning." There is only one, noncommittal line in *Profils du Zaire* about the Mulelist rebellion. But (unlike Lumumba) he gets a photograph, and it is a big one. It shows a smiling, gap-toothed African—in jacket and tie.

To Joseph Conrad, Stanleyville—in 1890 the Stanley Falls station—was the heart of darkness. It was there, in Conrad's story, that Kurtz reigned, the ivory agent degraded from idealism to savagery, taken back to the earliest ages of man, by wilderness, solitude and power, his house surrounded by impaled human heads. Seventy years later, at this bend in the river, something like Conrad's fantasy came to pass. But the man with "the inconceivable mystery of a soul that knew no restraint, no faith, and no fear" was black, and not white; and he had been maddened not by contact with wilderness and primitivism, but with the civilization established by those pioneers who now lie on Mont Ngaliema, above the Kinshasa rapids.

Mobutu embodies these African contradictions and, by the grandeur of his kingship, appears to ennoble them. He is, for all his stylishness, the great African nihilist, though his way is not the way of blood. He is the man "young but palpitating with wisdom and dynamism"— this is from a University of Zaire publication—who, during the dark days of secessions and rebellions, "thought through to the heart of the problem" and arrived at his especial illumination: the need for "authenticity," "I no longer have a borrowed conscience. I no longer have a

borrowed soul. I no longer speak a borrowed language."
He will bring back ancestral ways and reverences; he will
re-create that pure, logical world.

"Our religion is based on a belief in God the creator
and the worship of our ancestors." This is what a minister
told teachers the other day. "Our dead parents are living;
it is they who protect us and intercede for us." No need
now for the Christian saints, or Christianity. Christ was the
prophet of the Jews and he is dead. Mobutu is the prophet
of the Africans. "This prophet rouses us from our torpor,
and has delivered us from our mental alienation. He teaches
us to love one another." In public places the crucifix should
be replaced by the image of the messiah, just as in China
the portrait of Mao is honored everywhere. And Mobutu's
glorious mother, Mama Yemo, should also be honored, as
the Holy Virgin was honored.

So Mobutism becomes the African way out. The dances
and songs of Africa, so many of them religious in origin,
are now officially known as *séances d'animation* and are made
to serve the new cult; the dancers wear cloths stamped
with Mobutu's image. Old rituals, absorbed into the new,
their setting now not the village but the television studio,
the palace, the conference hall, appear to have been given
fresh dignity. African awakes! And, in all things, Mobutu
offers himself as the African substitute. At the end of January Mobutu told the Afro-American conference at Kinshasa (sponsored by the Ford and Carnegie foundations):

"Karl Marx is a great thinker whom I respect." But Marx wasn't always right; he was wrong, for instance, about the beneficial effects of colonialism. "The teachings of Karl Marx were addressed to his society. The teachings of Mobutu are addressed to the people of Zaire."

In Africa such comparisons, when they are made, have to be unabashed: African needs are great. And Mobutism is so wrapped up in the glory of Mobutu's kingship—the new palaces (the maharaja-style palace at Kisangani confiscated from Mr. Nasser, an old Indian settler), the presidential park at Mont Ngaliema (where Africans walk with foreigners on Sundays and pretend to be amused by the monkeys), the presidential domain at Nsele (open to faithful members of the party: and passengers on the steamer and the barges rush to look), the state visits abroad, intensively photographed, the miracle of the peace Mobutu has brought to the country, the near-absence of policemen in the towns—so glorious are the manifestations of Mobutu's kingship, so good are the words of the king, who proclaims himself a friend of the poor and, as a cook's son, one of the *petit peuple,* that all the contradictions of Africa appear to have been resolved and to have been turned into a kind of power.

But the contradictions remain, and are now sometimes heightened. The newspapers carry articles about science and medicine. But a doctor, who now feels he can say that he cures "when God and the ancestors wish," tells a newspaper that sterility is either hereditary or caused by a curse; and another newspaper gives publicity to a healer, a man made confident by the revolution, who has an infallible cure for piles, an "exclusive" secret given him by the ancestors. Agriculture must be modernized, the people must be fed better; but, in the name of authenticity, a doctor warns that babies should on no account be fed on imported foods; traditional foods, like caterpillars and green leaves, are best. The industrialized West is decadent and collapsing; Zaire must rid herself of the plagues of the consumer society, the egoism and individualism exported by industrial civilization. But in the year 2000, according to a university writer in *Elima,* Zaire might herself be booming, with great cities, a population of "probably" 71,933,851, and a prodigious manufacturing capacity. Western Europe will be in its "post-industrial" decadence; Russia, Eastern Europe and the Indian subcontinent will form one bloc; Arab oil will be exhausted; and Zaire (and Africa) should have her day, attracting investment from developed countries (obviously those not in decadence), importing factories whole.

So the borrowed ideas—about colonialism and alien-ation, the consumer society and the decline of the West—are made to serve the African cult of authenticity; and the dream of an ancestral past restored is allied to a dream of a future of magical power. The confusion is not new, and is not peculiar to Zaire. Fantasies like this animated some slave revolts in the West Indies; and today, in Jamaica, at the university, there are people who feel that Negro redemption and Negro power can only come about through a return to African ways. The dead Duvalier of Haiti is admired for his Africanness; a writer speaks with unconscious irony of the Negro's need for a "purifying" period of poverty (unwittingly echoing Duvalier's "It is the destiny of the people of Haiti to suffer"); and there are people who, sufficiently far away from the slaughter ground of Uganda, find in Amin's African nihilism a proof of African power.

It is lunacy, despair. In the February 7th issue of *Jeune Afrique*—miraculously on sale in Kinshasa—a French African writer, Seydou Lamine, examines the contradictions of African fantasy and speaks of "the alibi of the past." Mightn't this talk of Africanness, he asks, be a "myth" which the "princes" of Africa now use to strengthen their own position? "For many, authenticity and Negroness [*la négrité*] are only words that stand for the despair and powerlessness of the man of Africa faced with the discouraging immensity of his underdevelopment."

And even *Elima,* considering the general corruption, the jobs not done, the breakdown of municipal administration in Kinshasa, the uncleared garbage, the canals not disinfected (though the taxis are, regularly, for the one-zaire fee), the vandalized public television sets and telephone booths, even *Elima* finds it hard on some days to blame the colonial past for these signs of egoism. "We are wrong to consider the word 'underdevelopment' only in its economic aspects. We have to understand that there is a type of underdevelopment that issues out of the habits of a people and their attitudes to life and society."

Mobutism, *Elima* suggests, will combat this "mental plague." But it is no secret that, in spite of its talk of "man," in spite of its lilting national anthem called the *Zairoise ("Paix, justice et travail")*, Mobutism honors only one man: the chief, the king. He alone has to be feared and loved. How—away from this worship—does a new attitude to life and society begin? Recently in Kinshasa a number of people were arrested for some reason and taken to Makala jail: lavatoryless concrete blocks behind a whitewashed wall, marked near the gateway DISCIPLINE AVANT TOUT. The people arrested couldn't fit easily into the cell, and a Land Rover was used to close the door. In the morning many were found crushed or suffocated.

Not cruelty, just thoughtlessness: the visitor has to learn to accommodate himself to Zaire. The presidential domain at Nsele (where Muhammad Ali trained) is such a waste, at once extravagant and shoddy, with its over-furnished air-conditioned bungalows, its vast meeting halls, its VIP lounges (carpets, a fussiness of fringed Dralon, African art debased to furniture decoration). But Nsele can be looked at in another way. It speaks of the African need for African style and luxury; it speaks of the great African wound. The wound explains the harassment of

foreign settlers, the nationalizations. But the nationalizations are petty and bogus; they have often turned out
to be a form of pillage and are part of no creative plan;
they are as short-sighted, self-wounding and nihilistic as
they appear, a dismantling of what remains of the Belgian-
created state. So the visitor swings from mood to mood,
and one reaction cancels out another.

Where, in Kinshasa, where so many people "shadow"
jobs, and so many jobs are artificial and political, part of
an artificial administration, where does the sense of responsibility, society, the state, begin? A city of two million,
with almost no transport, with no industries (save for those
assembly plants, sited, as in so many "developing" countries, on the road from the airport to the capital), a city
detached from the rest of the country, existing only because
the Belgians built it and today almost without a point. It
doesn't have to work; it can be allowed to look after itself.
Already at night, a more enduring kind of bush life seems
to return to central Kinshasa, when the watchmen (who
also shadow their jobs: they will protect nothing) bar off
their territory, using whatever industrial junk there is to
hand, light fires on the broken pavements, cook their little messes and go to sleep. When it is hot the gutters
smell; in the rain the streets are flooded. And the unregu-
lated city spreads: meandering black rivulets of filth in
unpaved alleys, middens beside the highways, children,
discarded motorcar tires, a multitude of little stalls, and

everywhere, in free spaces, plantings of sugarcane and maize: subsistence agriculture in the town, a remnant of bush life.

But at the end of one highway there is the university. It is said to have gone down. But the students are bright and friendly. They have come from the bush, but already they can talk of Stendhal and Fanon; they have the enthusiasm of people to whom everything is new; and they feel, too, that with the economic collapse of the West (of which the newspapers talk every day) the tide is running Africa's way. The enthusiasm deserves a better-equipped country. It seems possible that many of these students, awakening to ideas, history, a knowledge of injustice and a sense of their own dignity, will find themselves unsupported by their society, and can only awaken to pain. But no. For most there will be jobs in the government; and already they are Mobutists to a man. Already the African way ahead is known; already inquiry is restricted; and Mobutu himself has warned that the most alienated people in Zaire are the intellectuals.

So Mobutism simplifies the world, the concept of responsibility and the state, and simplifies people. Zaire's accession to power and glory has been made to appear so easy; the plundering of the inherited Belgian state has been so easy, the confiscations and nationalizations, the distribution of big shadow jobs. Creativity itself now begins to appear as something that might be looted, brought into being by decree.

Zaire has her music and dance. To complete her glory, Zaire needs a literature; other African countries have literatures. The trouble, *Elima* says in a full-page Sunday article, is that far too many people who haven't written a line and sometimes can't even speak correctly have been going here and there and passing themselves off as Zairois writers, shaming the country. That will now stop; the bogus literary "circles" will be replaced by official literary "salons"; and they must set to work right away. In two months the president will be going to Paris. The whole world will be watching, and it is important that in these two months a work of Zairois literature be written and published. Other works should be produced for the Lagos Festival of Negro Arts at the end of the year. And it seems likely, from the tone of the *Elima* article, that it is Mobutu who has spoken.

Mobutu speaks all the time. He no longer speaks in French but in Lingala, the local lingua franca, and transistors take his words to the deep bush. He speaks as the chief, and the people listen. They laugh constantly, and they applaud. It has been Mobutu's brilliant idea to give the people of Zaire what they have not had and what they have long needed: an African king. The king expresses all the dignity of his people; to possess a king is to share the king's dignity. The individual's responsibility—a possible source of despair, in the abjectness of Africa—is lessened. All that is required is obedience, and obedience is easy.

Mobutu proclaims his simple origins. He is a *citoyen* like everyone else. And Mama Mobutu, Mobutu's wife, loves the poor. She runs a center for deprived girls, and they devote themselves to agriculture and to making medallions of the king, which the loyal will wear: there can never be too many images of Mobutu in Zaire. The king's little magnanimities are cherished by a people little used to magnanimity. Many Zairois will tell you that a hospital steamer now serves the river villages. But it is where Mobutu appears to be most extravagant that he satisfies his people most. The king's mother is to be honored; and she was a simple woman of Africa. Pilgrimages are announced to places connected with the king's life; and the disregarded bush of Africa becomes sacred again.

The newspapers, diluting the language of Fanon and Mao, speak every day of the revolution and the radicalization of the revolution. But this is what the revolution is about: the kingship. In Zaire Mobutu is the news: his speeches, his receptions, the *marches de soutien,* the new appointments: court news. Actual events are small. The nationalization of a gaudy furniture shop in Kinshasa is big news, as is the revelation that there is no African on the board of a brewery. Anti-revolutionary activity, discovered by the "vigilance" of the people, has to do with crooked vendors in the market, an official using a government vehicle as a night taxi, someone else building a house where he shouldn't, some drunken members of the youth wing of the party wrecking the party Volkswagen at Kisangani. There is no news in Zaire because there is little new activity. Copper continues to be mined; the big dam at Inga continues to be built. Airports are being extended or constructed everywhere, but this doesn't mean that Air Zaire is booming: it is for the better policing of the country.

What looked obvious on the first day, but was then blurred by the reasonable-sounding words, turns out to be true. The kingship of Mobutu has become its own end. The inherited modern state is being dismantled, but it isn't important that the state should work. The bush works; the bush has always been self-sufficient. The administration, now the court, is something imposed, something unconnected with the true life of the country. The ideas of responsibility, the state and creativity are ideas brought by the visitor; they do not correspond, for all the mimicry of language, to African aspirations.

Mobutu's peace and his kingship are great achievements. But the kingship is sterile. The cult of the king already swamps the intellectual advance of a people who have barely emerged. The intellectual confusions of authenticity, that now give such an illusion of power, close up the world again and point to a future greater despair. Mobutu's power will inevitably be extinguished; but there can now be no going back on the principles of Mobutism. Mobutu has established the pattern for his successors; and they will find that African dependence is not less than it is now, nor the need for nihilistic assertion.

To arrive at this sense of a country trapped and static, eternally vulnerable, is to begin to have something of the African sense of the void. It is to begin to fall, in the African way, into a dream of a past—the vacancy of river and forest, the hut in the brown yard, the dugout—when the dead ancestors watched and protected, and the enemies were only men.

1975

Jack's Garden
from THE ENIGMA OF ARRIVAL

For the first four days it rained. I could hardly see where I was. Then it stopped raining and beyond the lawn and outbuildings in front of my cottage I saw fields with stripped trees on the boundaries of each field; and far away, depending on the light, glints of a little river, glints which sometimes appeared, oddly, to be above the level of the land.

The river was called the Avon; not the one connected with Shakespeare. Later—when the land had more meaning, when it had absorbed more of my life than the tropical street where I had grown up—I was able to think of the flat wet fields with the ditches as "water meadows" or "wet meadows," and the low smooth hills in the background, beyond the river, as "downs." But just then, after the rain, all that I saw—though I had been living in England for twenty years—were flat fields and a narrow river.

It was winter. This idea of winter and snow had always excited me; but in England the word had lost some of its romance for me, because the winters I had found in England had seldom been as extreme as I had imagined they would be when I was far away in my tropical island. I had experienced severe weather in other places—in Spain in January, in a skiing resort near Madrid; in India, in Simla in December, and in the high Himalayas in August. But in England this kind of weather hardly seemed to come. In England I wore the same kind of clothes all through the year; seldom wore a pullover; hardly needed an overcoat.

And though I knew that summers were sunny and that in winter the trees went bare and brushlike, as in the watercolors of Rowland Hilder, the year—so far as vegetation and even temperature went—was a blur to me. It was hard for me to distinguish one section or season from the other; I didn't associate flowers or the foliage of trees with any particular month. And yet I liked to look; I noticed everything, and could be moved by the beauty of trees and flowers and early sunny mornings and late light evenings. Winter was to me a time mainly of short days, and of electric lights everywhere at working hours; also a time when snow was a possibility.

If I say it was winter when I arrived at that house in the river valley, it is because I remember the mist, the four days of rain and mist that hid my surroundings from me and answered my anxiety at the time, anxiety about my work and this move to a new place, yet another of the many moves I had made in England.

It was winter, too, because I was worried about the cost of heating. In the cottage there was only electricity—more expensive than gas or oil. And the cottage was hard to heat. It was long and narrow; it was not far from the water meadows and the river; and the concrete floor was just a foot or so above the ground.

And then one afternoon it began to snow. Snow dusted the lawn in front of my cottage; dusted the bare branches of the trees; outlined disregarded things, outlined the empty, old-looking buildings around the lawn that I hadn't yet paid attention to or fully taken in; so that piece by piece, while I considered the falling snow, a rough picture of my setting built up around me.

Rabbits came out to play on the snow, or to feed. A mother rabbit, hunched, with three or four of her young. They were a different, dirty color on the snow. And this picture of the rabbits, or more particularly their new color, calls up or creates the other details of the winter's day: the late-afternoon snow light; the strange, empty houses around the lawn becoming white and distinct and more important. It also calls up the memory of the forest I thought I saw behind the whitening hedge against which the rabbits fed. The white lawn; the empty houses around it; the hedge to one side of the lawn, the gap in the hedge, a path; the forest beyond. I saw a forest. But it wasn't a forest really; it was only the old orchard at the back of the big house in whose grounds my cottage was.

I saw what I saw very clearly. But I didn't know what I was looking at. I had nothing to fit it into. I was still in a kind of limbo. There were certain things I knew, though. I knew the name of the town I had come to by the train. It was Salisbury. It was almost the first English town I had got to know, the first I had been given some idea of, from the reproduction of the Constable painting of Salisbury Cathedral in my third-standard reader. Far away in my tropical island, before I was ten. A four-color reproduction which I had thought the most beautiful picture I had ever seen. I knew that the house I had come to was in one of the river valleys near Salisbury.

Apart from the romance of the Constable reproduction, the knowledge I brought to my setting was linguistic. I knew that "avon" originally meant only river, just as "hound" originally just meant a dog, any kind of dog. And I knew that both elements of Waldenshaw—the name of the village and the manor in whose grounds I was—I knew that both "walden" and "shaw" meant wood. One further reason why, apart from the fairy-tale feel of the snow and the rabbits, I thought I saw a forest.

I also knew that the house was near Stonehenge. I knew there was a walk which took one near the stone circle; I knew that somewhere high up on this walk there was a viewing point. And when the rain stopped and the mist lifted, after those first four days, I went out one after-noon, looking for the walk and the view.

There was no village to speak of. I was glad of that. I would have been nervous to meet people. After all my time in England I still had that nervousness in a new place, that rawness of response, still felt myself to be in the other man's country, felt my strangeness, my solitude. And every excursion into a new part of the country—what for others might have been an adventure—was for me like a tearing at an old scab.

The narrow public road ran beside the dark, yew-screened grounds of the manor. Just beyond the road and the wire fence and the roadside scrub the down sloped sharply upwards. Stonehenge and the walk lay in that direc-tion. There would have been a lane or path leading off the public road. To find that lane or path, was I to turn left or right? There was no problem, really. You came to a lane if you turned left; you came to another lane if you turned right. Those two lanes met at Jack's cottage, or the old farm-yard where Jack's cottage was, in the valley over the hill.

Two ways to the cottage. Different ways: one was very old, and one was new. The old way was longer, flatter; it followed an old, wide, winding riverbed; it would have been used by carts in the old days. The new way—meant for machines—was steeper, up the hill and then directly down again.

You came to the old way if you turned left on the public road. This stretch of road was overhung by beeches. It ran on a ledge in the down just above the river; and then it dropped almost to the level of the river. A little settlement here, just a few houses. I noticed: a small old house of brick and flint with a fine portico; and, on the riverbank, very close to the water, a low, white-walled thatched cottage that was being "done up." (Years later that cottage was still being done up; half-used sacks of cement were still to be seen through the dusty windows.) Here, in this settlement, you turned off into the old way to Jack's cottage.

An asphalt lane led past half a dozen ordinary little houses, two or three of which carried—their only fanciful touch—the elaborate monogram of the owner or builder or designer, with the date, which was, surprisingly, a date from the war: 1944. The asphalt gave out, the narrow lane became rocky; then, entering a valley, became wide, with many flinty wheeled ruts separated by uneven strips of coarse, tufted grass. This valley felt old. To the left the steep slope shut out a further view. This slope was bare, without trees or scrub; below its smooth, thin covering of grass could be seen lines and stripes, like weals, suggesting many consecutive years of tilling a long time ago; suggesting also fortifications. The wide way twisted; the wide valley (possibly an ancient river course) which the way occupied then ran straight and far, bounded in the distance by the beginning of a low down. Jack's cottage and the farmyard were at the end of that straight way, where the way turned.

The other way to the cottage, the shorter, steeper, newer way, up from the main road and then down to the valley and the farmyard, was lined on the northern side with a windbreak, young beech trees protected by taller pines. At the top of the slope there was a modern, metal-walled barn; just a little way down on the other side there was a gap in the windbreak. This was the viewing point for Stonehenge: far away, small, not easy to see, not as easy as the luminous red or orange targets of the army firing ranges. And at the bottom of the slope, down the rocky, uneven lane beside the windbreak, were the derelict farm buildings and the still living row of agricultural cottages, one of which Jack lived in.

The downs all around were flinty and dry, whitish brown, whitish green. But on the wide way at the bottom, around the farm buildings, the ground was muddy and black. The tractor wheels had dug out irregular linear ponds in the black mud.

The first afternoon, when I reached the farm buildings, walking down the steep way, beside the windbreak, I had to ask the way to Stonehenge. From the viewing point at the top, it had seemed clear. But from that point down had risen against down, slope against slope; dips and paths had been hidden; and at the bottom, where mud and long puddles made walking difficult and made the spaces seem bigger, and there appeared to be many paths, some leading off the wide valley way, I was confused. Such a simple inquiry, though, in the emptiness; and I never forgot that on the first day I had asked someone the way. Was it Jack? I didn't take the person in; I was more concerned with the strangeness of the walk, my own strangeness, and the absurdity of my inquiry.

I was told to go round the farm buildings, to turn to the right, to stick to the wide main way, and to ignore all the tempting dry paths that led off the main way to the woods which lay on the other side, young woods that falsely suggested deep country, the beginning of forest.

So, past the mud around the cottages and the farmyard, past the mess of old timber and tangled old barbed wire and apparently abandoned pieces of farm machinery, I turned right. The wide muddy way became grassy, long wet grass. And soon, when I had left the farm buildings behind and felt myself walking in a wide, empty, old riverbed, the sense of space was overwhelming.

The grassy way, the old riverbed (as I thought), sloped up, so that the eye was led to the middle sky; and on either side were the slopes of the downs, widening out and up against the sky. On one side there were cattle; on the other side, beyond a pasture, a wide empty area, there were young pines, a little forest. The setting felt ancient; the impression was of space, unoccupied land, the beginning of things. There were no houses to be seen, only the wide grassy way, the sky above it, and the wide slopes on either side.

It was possible on this stretch of the walk to hold on to

the idea of emptiness. But when I got to the top of the grassy way and was on a level with the barrows and tumuli which dotted the high downs all around, and I looked down at Stonehenge, I saw also the firing ranges of Salisbury Plain and the many little neat houses of West Amesbury. The emptiness, the spaciousness through which I had felt myself walking was as much an illusion as the idea of forest behind the young pines. All around—and not far away—were roads and highways, with brightly colored trucks and cars like toys. Stonehenge, old barrows and tumuli outlined against the sky; the army firing ranges, West Amesbury. The old and the new; and, from a midway or a different time, the farmyard with Jack's cottage at the bottom of the valley.

Many of the farm buildings were no longer used. The barns and pens—red-brick walls, roofs of slate or clay tiles—around the muddy yard were in decay; and only occasionally in the pens were there cattle—sick cattle, enfeebled calves, isolated from the herd. Fallen tiles, holed roofs, rusted corrugated iron, bent metal, a pervading damp, the colors rust and brown and black, with a glittering or dead-green moss on the trampled, dung-softened mud of the pen yard: the isolation of the animals in that setting, like things themselves about to be discarded, was terrible.

Once there were cattle there that had suffered from some malformation. The breeding of these cattle had become so mechanical that the malformation appeared mechanical too, the mistakes of an industrial process. Curious additional lumps of flesh had grown at various places on the animals, as though these animals had been cast in a mold, a mold divided into two sections, and as though, at the joining of the molds, the cattle material, the mixture out of which the cattle were being cast, had leaked; and had hardened, matured into flesh, and had then developed hair with the black-and-white Frisian pattern of the rest of the cattle. There, in the ruined, abandoned, dungy, mossy farmyard, fresh now only with their own dung, they had stood, burdened in this puzzling way, with this extra cattle material hanging down their middles like a bull's dewlaps, like heavy curtains, waiting to be taken off to the slaughterhouse in the town.

Away from the old farm buildings, and down the wide flat way which I thought of as the old road to the farm and Jack's cottage, there were other remnants and ruins, relics of other efforts or lives. At the end of the wide way, to one side of it in tall grass, were flat shallow boxes, painted gray, set down in two rows. I was told later that they were or had been beehives. I was never told who it was who had kept the bees. Was it a farm worker, someone from the cottages, or was it someone more leisured, attempting a little business enterprise and then giving up and forgetting? Abandoned now, unexplained, the gray boxes that were worth no one's while to take away were a little mysterious in the unfenced openness.

On the other side of the wide droveway, its great curve round the farm buildings just beginning here, in the shelter of young trees and scrub there was an old green-and-yellow-and-red caravan in good condition, a brightly painted gypsy caravan of the old days (as I thought), looking as if its horses had been unhitched not long before. Another mystery; another carefully made thing abandoned; another piece of the past that no longer had a use but had not been thrown away. Like the antiquated, cumbersome pieces of farm machinery scattered and rusting about the farm buildings.

Midway down the straight wide way, far beyond the beehives and the caravan, was an old hayrick, with bales of hay stacked into a cottage-shaped structure and covered with old black plastic sheeting. The hay had grown old; out of its blackness there were green sprouts; the hay that had been carefully cut one summer and baled and stored was decaying, turning to manure. The hay of the farm was now stored in a modern open shed, a prefabricated structure which carried the printed name of the maker just below the apex of the roof. The shed had been erected just beyond the mess of the old farmyard—as though space would always be available, and nothing old need ever be built over. The hay in this shed was new, with a sweet, warm smell; and the bales unstacked into golden, clean, warm-smelling steps, which made me think of the story about spinning straw into gold and of refer-

ences in books with European settings to men sleeping
on straw in barns. That had never been comprehensible to
me in Trinidad, where grass was always freshly cut for cattle, always green, and never browned into hay. Now, in winter, at the bottom of this damp valley: high-stacked golden
hay bales, warm golden steps next to rutted black mud.

Not far from the decaying rick shaped like a hut or
cottage there were the remains of a true house, a house
with walls that might have been of flint and concrete. A
simple house, its walls perhaps without foundations, it
was now quite exposed. Ruined walls, roofless, around
bare earth—no sign of a stone or concrete floor. How
damp it felt! All around the plot the boundary trees—
sycamore or beech or oak—had grown tall, dwarfing the
house. Once they would have been barely noticeable, the
trees that, living on while the house had ceased to be,
now kept the ground chill and mossy and black and in
perpetual shadow. Smaller houses beside the public roads,
houses built by squatters in the last century, farm laborers
mainly, had established ownership rights for the builders
and their descendants. But here, beside the grassy droveway, in the middle of downs and fields and solitude, the
owner or the builder of the house had left nothing
behind; nothing had been established. Only the trees he
had planted had continued to grow.

Perhaps the house had been no more than a shepherd's
shelter. But that was only a guess. Shepherds' huts would

have been smaller; and the trees around the plot didn't speak of a shepherd's hut, didn't speak of a man lodging there for only a few nights at a time.

Sheep were no longer the main animals of the plain. I saw a sheep-shearing only once. It was done by a big man, an Australian, I was told, and the shearing was done in one of the old buildings—timber walls and a slate roof—at the side of the cottage row in which Jack lived. I saw the shearing by accident; I had heard nothing about it; it just happened at the time of my afternoon walk. But the shearing had clearly been news for some; the farm people and people from elsewhere as well had gathered to watch. A display of strength and speed, the fleecy animal lifted and shorn (and sometimes cut) at the same time, and then sent off, oddly naked—the ceremony was like something out of an old novel, perhaps by Hardy, or out of a Victorian country diary. And it was as though, then, the firing ranges of Salisbury Plain, and the vapor trails of military aircraft in the sky, and the army houses and the roaring highways didn't lie around us. As though, in that little spot around the farm buildings and Jack's cottage, time had stood still, and things were as they had been, for a little while. But the sheep-shearing was from the past. Like the old farm buildings. Like the caravan that wasn't going to move again. Like the barn where grain was no longer stored.

This barn had a high window with a projecting metal

bracket. Perhaps a pulley wheel and a chain or rope had been attached to this metal bracket to lift bales off the carts and wagons and then swing them through the high open window into the barn. There was a similar antique fixture in the town of Salisbury, at the upper level of what had been a well-known old grocery shop. It had survived or been allowed to live on as an antique, a trademark, something suited to an old town careful of its past. But what was an antique in the town was rubbish at the bottom of the hill. It was part of a barn that was crumbling winter by winter—the barn and the other dilapidated farm buildings no doubt allowed to survive because, in this protected area, planning regulations allowed new buildings to go up only where buildings existed.

And just as the modern prefabricated shed had replaced the old rotting hayrick, so—but far away, not a simple addition to the old farm buildings—the true barn was now at the top of the hill, beside the windbreak. It had galvanized tin walls; it would have been ratproof. There machinery caused everything to go; and the powerful trucks (not nowadays the wagons that might have used the flat droveway to the old barn at the bottom of the valley) climbed up the rocky lane from the public road and pulled into the concrete yard of the barn, and the spout from the barn poured the dusty grain into the deep trays of the trucks.

The straw was golden, warm; the grain was golden; but the dust that fell all around—on the concrete yard, the rocky lane, the pines and young beeches of the wind-break—the dust that fell after the grain had poured into the trays of the trucks was gray. At the side of the metal-walled barn, and below a metal spout, there was a conical mound of dust that had been winnowed by some mechanical means from the bigger conical mounds of grain in the barn. This dust—the mound firm at the base, wonderfully soft at the top—was very fine and gray, without a speck of gold.

New, this barn, with all its mechanical contrivances. But just next to it, across an unpaved muddy lane, was another ruin: a wartime bunker, a mound planted over with sycamores, for concealment, and with a metal ventilator sticking out oddly now among the trunks of the grown trees. The sycamores would have been planted at least twenty-five years before; but they had been planted close together, and they still looked young.

Jack lived among ruins, among superseded things. But that way of looking came to me later, has come to me with greater force now, with the writing. It wasn't the idea that came to me when I first went out walking.

That idea of ruin and dereliction, of out-of-placeness, was something I felt about myself, attached to myself: a man from another hemisphere, another background, coming to rest in middle life in the cottage of a half-neglected estate, an estate full of reminders of its Edwardian past, with few connections with the present. An oddity among the estates and big houses of the valley, and I a further oddity in its grounds. I felt unanchored and strange. Everything I saw in those early days, as I took my surroundings in, everything I saw on my daily walk, beside the windbreak or along the wide grassy way, made that feeling more acute. I felt that my presence in that old valley was part of something like an upheaval, a change in the course of the history of the country.

Jack himself, however, I considered to be part of the view. I saw his life as genuine, rooted, fitting: man fitting the landscape. I saw him as a remnant of the past (the undoing of which my own presence portended). It did not occur to me, when I first went walking and saw only the view, took what I saw as things of that walk, things that one might see in the countryside near Salisbury, immemorial, appropriate things, it did not occur to me that Jack was living in the middle of junk, among the ruins of nearly a century; that the past around his cottage might not have been his past; that he might at some stage have been a newcomer to the valley; that his style of life might have been a matter of choice, a conscious act; that out of the little piece of earth which had come to him with his farm worker's cottage (one of a row of three) he had created a special land for himself, a garden, where (though surrounded by ruins, reminders of vanished lives) he was more than content to live out his life and where, as in a version of a book of hours, he celebrated the seasons.

I saw him as a remnant. Not far away, among the ancient barrows and tumuli, were the firing ranges and the army training grounds of Salisbury Plain. There was a story that because of the absence of people in those military areas, because of the purely military uses to which the land had been put for so long, and contrary to what one might expect after the explosions and mock warfare, there survived on the plain some kinds of butterflies that had vanished in more populated parts. And I thought that in some such fashion, in the wide droveway at the bottom of the valley, accidentally preserved from people, traffic and the military, Jack like the butterflies had survived.

I saw things slowly; they emerged slowly. It was not Jack whom I first noticed on my walks. It was Jack's father-in-law. And it was the father-in-law—rather than Jack—who seemed a figure of literature in that ancient landscape. He seemed a Wordsworthian figure: bent, exaggeratedly bent, going gravely about his peasant tasks, as if in an immense Lake District solitude.

He walked very slowly, the bent old man; he did everything very deliberately. He had worked out his own paths across the downs and he stuck to them. You could follow these paths even across barbed-wire fences, by the blue plastic sacks (originally containing fertilizer) which the old man had rolled around the barbed wire and then tied very tightly with red nylon string, working with a thoroughness that matched his pace and deliberateness to create these safe padded places where he could cross below the barbed wire or climb over it.

The old man first, then. And, after him, the garden, the garden in the midst of superseded things. It was Jack's garden that made me notice Jack—the people in the other cottages I never got to know, couldn't recognize, never knew when they moved in or moved out. But it took some time to see the garden. So many weeks, so many walks between the whitish chalk and flint hills up to the level of the barrows to look down at Stonehenge, so many walks just looking for hares—it took some time before, with the beginning of my new awareness of the seasons, I noticed the garden. Until then it had simply been there, something on the walk, a marker, not to be specially noticed. And yet I loved landscape, trees, flowers, clouds, and was responsive to changes of light and temperature.

I noticed his hedge first of all. It was well clipped, tight in the middle, but ragged in places at ground level. I felt, from the clipping, that the gardener would have liked that hedge to be tight all over, to be as complete as a wall of brick or timber or some kind of man-fashioned material. The hedge marked the boundary between Jack's fruit and flower garden and the droveway, which was very wide here, bare ground around the cottages and the farm buildings, and nearly always soft or muddy. In winter the long puddles reflected the sky between black, tractor-marked mud. For a few days in summer that black mud dried out, turned hard and white and dusty. So for a few days in the summer the hedge that ran the length of the garden that Jack possessed with his cottage was white with chalk dust for a foot or so above the ground; in winter it was spattered with mud, drying out white or gray.

The hedge hid nothing. As you came down the hill with the windbreak you could see it all. The old rust-and-black farm buildings in the background; the gray-plastered cottages in front of them; the ground or gardens in front of the cottages; the emptiness or no-man's-land in front of the cottage grounds or gardens. And beside Jack's garden, Jack's hedge: a little wall of mud-spattered green, abrupt in the openness of the droveway, like a vestige, a memory of another kind of house and garden and street, a token of something more complete, more ideal.

Technically, the gardens were at the front of the cottages. In fact, by long use, the back of the cottages had become the front; and the front gardens had really become back gardens. But Jack, with the same instinct that made him grow and carefully clip (and also abruptly end) that hedge beside the droveway, treated his garden like a front garden. A paved path with a border of some sort ran from his "front" door all the way down the middle of his garden. This should have led to a gate, a pavement, a street.

There was a gate; but this gate, set in a wide-meshed wire-netting fence, led only to a wire-fenced patch of earth which was forked over every year: it was here that Jack planted out his annuals. In front of this was the empty area, the no-man's-land between droveway and the beginning of the cultivated down. Jack's ducks and geese had their sheds in that area, which was messy with dung and feathers. Though they were not penned in, the ducks and geese never strayed far; they just walked back and forth across the droveway.

Hedge, garden, planting-out bed for annuals, a plot for ducks and geese; and beyond that, beyond the ground reserved for the other two cottages, just where the land began to slope up to the farm's machine-cultivated fields, was the area where Jack grew his vegetables.

Every piece of ground was separate. Jack didn't see his setting as a whole. But he saw its component parts very clearly; and everything he tended answered the special idea he had of that thing. The hedge was regularly clipped, the garden was beautiful and clean and full of changing color and the goose plot was dirty, with roughly built sheds and enamel basins and bowls and discarded earthenware sinks. Like a medieval village in miniature, all the various pieces of the garden Jack had established around the old farm buildings. This was Jack's style, and it was this that suggested to me (falsely, as I got to know soon enough) the remnant of an old peasantry, surviving here like the butterflies among the explosions of Salisbury Plain, surviving somehow industrial revolution, deserted villages, railways and the establishing of the great agricultural estates in the valley.

So much of this I saw with the literary eye, or with the aid of literature. A stranger here, with the nerves of the stranger, and yet with a knowledge of the language and the history of the language and the writing, I could find a special kind of past in what I saw; with a part of my mind I could admit fantasy.

I heard on the radio one morning that in the days of the Roman Empire geese could be walked to market all the way from the province of Gaul to Rome. After this, the high-headed, dung-dropping geese that strutted across the muddy, rutted way at the bottom of the valley and could be quite aggressive at times—Jack's geese—developed a kind of historical life for me, something that went beyond the idea of medieval peasantry, old English country ways and the drawings of geese in children's books. And when one year, longing for Shakespeare, longing to be put in touch with the early language, I returned to *King Lear* for the first time for more than twenty years, and read in Kent's railing speech, "Goose, if I had you upon Sarum Plain, I'd drive ye cackling home to Camelot," the words were quite clear to me. Sarum Plain, Salisbury Plain; Camelot, Winchester—just twenty miles away. And I felt that with the help of Jack's geese—creatures with perhaps an antiquity in the droveway lands that Jack would not have guessed—I had arrived at an understanding of something in *King Lear* which, according to the editor of the text I read, commentators had found obscure.

The solitude of the walk, the emptiness of that stretch of the downs, enabled me to surrender to my way of looking, to indulge my linguistic or historical fantasies; and enable me, at the same time, to shed the nerves of being a stranger in England. Accident—the shape of the fields, perhaps, the alignment of paths and modern roads, the needs of the military—had isolated this little region; and I had this historical part of England to myself when I went walking.

Daily I walked in the wide grassy way between the flint slopes, past chalk valleys rubbled white and looking sometimes like a Himalayan valley strewn in midsummer with old, gritted snow. Daily I saw the mounds that had been raised so many centuries before. The number of these mounds! They lay all around. From a certain height they were outlined against the sky and looked like pimples on the land. In the beginning I liked to tramp over the mounds that were more or less on my walk. The grass on these mounds was coarse; it was long-bladed, pale in color and grew in ankle-turning tufts or clumps. The trees, where they existed, were wind-beaten and stunted.

I picked my way up and down and around each mound; I wanted in those early days to leave no accessible mound unlooked at, feeling that if I looked hard enough and long enough I might arrive, not at an understanding of the religious mystery, but at an appreciation of the labor.

Daily I walked in the wide grassy way—perhaps in the old days a processional way. Daily I climbed up from the bottom of the valley to the crest of the way and the view: the stone circles directly ahead, down below, but still far away: gray against green, and sometimes lit up by the sun. Going up the grassy way (and though willing to admit that the true processional path might have been elsewhere) I never ceased to imagine myself a man of those bygone times, climbing up to have this confirmation that all was well with the world.

There was a main road on either side of the Henge. On those two roads trucks and vans and cars were like toys. At the foot of the Henge there was the tourist crowd—not very noticeable, not as noticeable as one might imagine from the fairground atmosphere around the stones when you actually went to them. The tourist crowd, from this distance, was noticeable only because of the red dress or coat that some of the women wore. That color red among the visitors to Stonehenge was something that I never failed to see; always someone in red, among the little figures.

And in spite of that crowd, and the highways, and the artillery ranges (with their fluorescent or semi-luminous targets), my sense of antiquity, my feeling for the age of the earth and the oldness of man's possession of it, was always with me. A vast sacred burial ground, bounded by the sky—of what activity those barrows and tumuli spoke, what numbers, what organization, what busyness in these now virtually empty downs! That sense of antiquity gave another scale to the activities around one. But at the same time—from this height, and with that wide view—there was a feeling of continuity.

So the idea of antiquity, at once diminishing and ennobling the current activities of men, as well as the ideas of literature, enveloped this world which—surrounded by highways and army barracks though it was, and with the very clouds in the sky sometimes seeded by the vapor trails of busy military airplanes—came to me as a lucky find of the solitude in which on many afternoons I found myself.

Larkhill was the name of the army artillery school. In my first or second year there was something like a fair or open day there when, in the presence of the families of the soldiers, guns were fired off. But the lark hill I looked for on my walk was the hill with ancient barrows where literally larks bred, and behaved like the larks of poetry. "And drown'd in yonder living blue the lark becomes a sightless song." It was true: the birds rose and rose, in almost vertical flight. I suppose I had heard larks before. But these were the first larks I noticed, the first I watched and listened to. They were another lucky find of my solitude, another unexpected gift.

And that became my mood. When I grew to see the wild roses and hawthorn on my walk, I didn't see the windbreak they grew beside as a sign of the big landowners who had left their mark on the solitude, had preserved it, had planted the woods in certain places (in imitation, it was said, of the positions at the battle of Trafalgar—or was it Waterloo?), I didn't think of the landowners. My mood was purer: I thought of these single-petaled roses and sweet-smelling blossoms at the side of the road as wild and natural growths.

One autumn day—the days shortening, filling me with thoughts of winter pleasures, fires and evening lights and books—one autumn day I felt something like a craving to read of winter in *Sir Gawain and the Green Knight*, a poem I had read more than twenty years before at Oxford as part of the Middle English course. The hips and the haws beside the windbreak, the red berries of this dead but warm time of year, made me want to read again about the winter journey in that old poem. And I read the poem on the bus back from Salisbury, where I had gone to buy it. So in tune with the landscape had I become, in that solitude, for the first time in England.

Of literature and antiquity and the landscape Jack and his garden and his geese and cottage and his father-in-law seemed emanations.

THE BOMOH'S SON

The Bomoh—healer, or shaman, or magic-man—was a year old older than the century. He was of mixed Chinese and Indonesian parentage. His father had left China towards the end of the nineteenth century, part of the spilling out of the poor and unprotected from the collapsing empire; and he had fetched up in one of the islands of the Indonesian archipelago, at that time ruled by the Dutch. There he had found some kind of footing, and he had married (or as good as married) an Indonesian woman. They had nine sons.

They were very poor. They moved at some point to a northern state in what was then British-ruled Malaya. The eighth son hardly had a childhood. He went out to work when he was quite young. When he was thirteen or fourteen he was driving a truck. Life was not easy; and at about this time the mystical, Indonesian side of the boy's personality began to assert itself. He became aware of his powers, and he began to train as a bomoh. There would have been a teacher or encourager of some sort, but I didn't ask about the teacher, and wasn't told.

This training as a bomoh would have begun in 1914–15. (While, far away, Europe was fighting the great war that indirectly weakened the British and Dutch empires in Asia; and, a little nearer home, Gandhi, after his twenty years in South Africa, was going back to India with his very special political-social-religious ideas.) The boy or young man learned very fast. He became a full bomoh when he was seventeen; and he practiced for nearly seventy years. He had a big following, and he had disciples. There were certain things he couldn't do when he became physically infirm, but his powers as a bomoh never failed him.

He married twice, to two Malay Chinese sisters, with five years between the marriages. He had seventeen children altogether, and they all lived in the same house.

Rashid was the bomoh's eighth son. He was born in 1955. He was sent to good local schools from the start; and in his eighteenth year—with every kind of tenderness for his father's feelings, and every kind of respect for his father's powers as a bomoh—Rashid began to turn away from his father's magical practices, and the rituals of the house. With education and self-awareness Rashid had begun to feel the kind of philosophical and spiritual need that Philip, the Chinese Christian convert, felt; and, indeed, for some time, picking up and repeating what he had heard from some friends at school, Rashid talked and behaved as a Christian, even at home.

Then he discovered Islam and the Koran, and he stayed there. He became a Muslim in his own mind, without being formally converted, and he took the Arab name of Rashid. He had started and dropped more than one career since then. Now he was a successful corporate lawyer, close to people with power. He was only forty. He had traveled far and fast, like the country. He had lived in, or had access to, many different spiritual worlds.

People brought all kinds of problems to his father, Rashid said. Payment was often in kind, four or five chickens, fruit; and it wasn't like settling a bill. Payment, once it started, went on as a regular voluntary tribute.

People came simply to be blessed, or to be cured of pains, or to have amulets blessed. Rashid remembered that once a famous local martial arts man, an elderly man, an exponent of jujitsu, came and knelt before his father and asked to be granted inner strength. The bomoh was known for his great strength. He was short, five feet four and a half inches, but well built. He could bend six-inch nails between his index finger and thumb, without having to go into a trance, which was what he normally had to do when he dealt with people's problems.

When he was in this trance people who wanted to be blessed knelt before him, and he touched them on the forehead, the shoulders, the solar plexus. Then he made them turn round and he touched them on the back of the head and the shoulders. When people were in pain he touched them on the part of the body that hurt.

Every year the bomoh's followers made a special pilgrimage to the bomoh's house and brought amulets to be blessed. These followers were of all communities and all classes, rich, poor, educated, ordinary. Rashid as a child of eight remembered hearing many languages during one of these pilgrimages: English, Malay, Hokkien Chinese, Baba or Chinese Malay.

The bomoh would go into a trance and in this trance he would take off his shirt. He would start shivering, because at that moment he would be focused in his trance on the snow deity, one of the three deities from whom he drew his powers. His assistants would hand him a bundle of flaming joss sticks. He needed the flames to warm himself, and he would appear to be outlining his body with the joss sticks. He would do this for a minute or so. When he was sufficiently warmed, he passed the sticks back to his assistants. They would then dress him in his special shirt and cover him with his cloak. The shirt was important; only the bomoh could wear it; he had blessed it on the altar of the shrine.

When he sat down his assistants gave him a glass of water. He would speak some incantations, blow on the water, drink it and spew it out. His sword would then be passed to him. This was a real sword, five feet long and double-edged. He would stick out his tongue, and use the sword to make a deep enough incision in his tongue for the blood to flow. The yellow slips of paper for the amulets would be ready. His assistants would pass him the slips one by one and he would drip blood from his tongue on each slip. He would keep on blessing slips in this way, losing blood all the time, until Rashid's mother said, "That's enough." By then he might have blessed a hundred slips.

When the sword was put away he would be covered up and, still in a trance, he would start giving his consultations. Women wanted to know whether they would get husbands, men whether they would get mistresses. Women who were being badly treated by their husbands wanted to know what they should do. Mothers or fathers wanted to know about those of their children who had gone astray.

The bomoh would speak in a language Rashid didn't understand. This was the special Javanese the bomoh had brought from the Indonesian island where he was born. He also spoke in Mandarin. It was only on these occasions, and in that trance, that Rashid's father spoke Mandarin.

The sword was special. It was the bomoh's own. An assistant went into a trance one day and tried to use the sword to cut his tongue. The sword wouldn't cut. When the bomoh was old, though, he allowed his tongue to be cut with the sword by one of his assistants. (But Rashid's language was ambiguous. I wasn't sure, when I looked at my notes some time later, whether the assistants cut their own tongues, or used the sword to cut the bomoh's tongue.)

The assistants were the bomoh's disciples. They didn't live in the house, but they were at the bomoh's beck and call. They came to the house every day, and they had to work. One of the things they did was to clean the altar. They were not paid. They were in no way the bomoh's employees. In fact, they had to bring offerings to the bomoh. Sometimes they even offered money—which the bomoh refused.

There were no statues on the altar. There was only a yellow cloth, with representations of the bomoh's three deities on a triangle: the snow-mountain god at the peak, with the deities of fire and sword at the base. Snow, fire, sword: the bomoh's ritual followed that sequence. He told his children on many occasions that he had masters of some kind. He had a master in China and another in

Indonesia, and (just as his followers came in pilgrimage to him once a year) he regularly made his own pilgrimage to these masters. He did so by astro-traveling. Rashid never doubted what his father said; he could find no other way of explaining his father's manifest powers.

The bomoh's wives—Rashid's mother and his aunt—were Baba-Nonya, overseas Straits Chinese, people of Chinese origin who had adopted Malay culture and the Malay language. The food in the house was Baba food, Malay-Chinese food, very spicy, and they ate with their hands. They didn't use chopsticks.

Rashid's mother, Chinese though she was, worshiped a Malay ancestor, the datuk. Many other Babas did that. Offerings to this datuk were made on the altar by Rashid's mother. The offerings were of Malay-style food: *rendang ayam*, curried chicken, *rendang daging*, curried beef, sticky rice: food to be eaten with the hands.

Once a month everybody in the house would have his cheeks pierced with a steel needle by the bomoh. This cheek-piercing was done as a form of purification. There was a different needle for everyone; the older the child, the longer and thicker the needle. The child whose cheek was pierced first would have to endure it the longest: the needle would stay in until everyone's cheeks were done. Sometimes, on special occasions, photographs were taken of the family, the seventeen children and the mothers, all with needles in their cheeks.

Up to the end of the second war the bomoh and his family lived in a kampung in a kampung-style house. Afterwards they moved to a resettled area, to a two-story terrace house. This was the house that Rashid had grown up in. There were three bedrooms upstairs and one bedroom downstairs. Rashid's mother and one or two of his sisters were in the room downstairs. Rashid's grandmother was in one room upstairs, with all the other girls. An uncle and his whole family lived in one room. All the boys slept on the landing. At any one time twenty people could be found living in the tiny house. And, with all of that, the bomoh practiced his profession downstairs, in the living room, which was also the temple.

The bomoh's powers were known in the neighborhood, and people were careful not to cross the family. As an aspect of his success, the bomoh also had a certain social standing in the community, and he was concerned to live up to it. He was particular about his dress when, relaxing from his bomoh work, he went out, as he sometimes did, to his Chinese clan clubs in the town. He dressed in the colonial way then, in a suit and with a bow tie. He would have a game of cards, and an occasional pipe of opium. One of the bomoh's brothers was an opium addict, and died from his addiction. But the bomoh was not an addict.

———

The bomoh had never gone to school. He alone knew how much he had suffered because of that as a child and young man, in that far-off time before and during the First World War. And now, in a changed world, he wanted all his children, daughters as well as sons, to be properly educated. He did the best he could for all of them.

Rashid was sent to a local primary school, and then to one of the most reputed colonial secondary schools in the district. Rashid didn't say it, but he would have known when he got to the secondary school that he was in another sphere. At home Rashid was proud of his father's powers, and liked them to be talked about locally; but he never talked about them at the secondary school. He never thought to "brag"—he used the schoolboy word—about his father there.

It was at this school that Rashid became aware of other religions. A friendly Tamil boy engaged him one day in "a very basic discussion" about big issues. The Tamil boy said, "Look at Hitler. Look at all those brutalities. You think these people are going to go scot free when they die? And who do you think will punish them? God will punish them. You think all of us are here without any purpose?"

The Tamil boy was a Christian. He didn't push his faith too hard at Rashid. He was just very friendly, and it was because of this boy that Rashid joined a school Bible class. At the same time Rashid began reading the King

James Bible. He liked the language, the pace of the stories, the movement. Other Chinese boys were doing the same thing. The Chinese boys were Buddhists, like Rashid; but they wanted more than they got from the Buddhism of their parents.

Rashid's little terrace house was full of rituals, with his father's temple downstairs, its festivities, the annual pilgrimage, and his mother's daily worship of her Malay datuk. But these rituals couldn't give answers to the bigger questions that Rashid was now beginning to have. His father's three deities didn't offer anything like "the ecumenical love" (the words were Rashid's) he was discovering in Christianity. "Ecumenical love": it was like the idea of grace that had overwhelmed Philip, the Chinese Christian convert. The deities of snow, fire and sword, and the temple rituals, offered Rashid no comparable philosophy, no "big picture." What happened in his father's temple was private. People just came there day after day to his father's temple with their practical problems.

And Rashid couldn't question his father about what he did. It was inconceivable, for instance, that he should ask his father whether God existed. His father was a bomoh; he had mystical powers. To question him about religion, to express doubt, would be to show disrespect, and that was the last thing Rashid wanted to do.

One of Rashid's brothers was more than halfway to being a Christian. He was going to church regularly. And

Rashid was going to the school Bible class. Sometimes at home, in the living room of the terrace house, where the temple altar was, they sang hymns together in the evenings. The bomoh might then be relaxing, watching television. The hymn-singing in his temple didn't worry him; he paid no attention.

At school Rashid and the Tamil boy had many talks about Jesus and the Trinity. Rashid wasn't actually converted, but he went around saying to people, "Why don't you start reading the Bible?" He preached at them the way the Tamil boy had preached at him. He talked to them about the purpose of life.

He did this to one of the bright girls at the school. The girl was a Pathan; Rashid was attracted to her. She said to him, "Have you ever read the Koran?"

He was prejudiced against Islam at that time. He thought of it as a backward religion; he associated it with Malays, whom at that time he considered a backward people. But he wanted to have something to talk to the girl about. So he began reading the Koran, in the Marmaduke Pickthall translation. He was fascinated by the introduction to the opening chapter; he thought it the equivalent of the Lord's Prayer. He liked, too, the constant reference to God as the Most Beneficient and the Most Merciful. This went against the idea he had of Islam and the sword.

But he had doubts. He didn't like the idea of polygamy

and what he could gather from his reading about the position of women in Islam. He asked the Pathan girl why the Prophet had married more than four wives, and the Pathan girl couldn't answer. Still, he kept on reading the Koran, and it began to appeal to his heart. He felt humbled by it. He liked the repeated references to God's guidance and man's need of it. "Show me the straight path": that, the fifth line of the opening chapter, went deep into him.

He began thinking of himself as a Muslim. To be a Muslim was to bear witness that there was no God but God, and the Prophet was his messenger. This should have created problems in his own mind about his father's practices as a bomoh. But it didn't. Rashid never associated religion with what his father did.

He was still seeing the Pathan girl. To him she was a living Muslim, an exemplar, and he began to follow her dietary habits. He was able now to recite Koranic verses. He didn't think it was enough for him; he thought he should read the Koran properly, in Arabic. He set himself to learn the Malay Arabic script; it took him two years to do sight reading.

By this time there was worry about him at home. Rashid's parents didn't like it when he refused to touch pork and refused to hold the joss sticks and perform rituals before the altar. He refused to eat cooked food and even fruit that had been offered up on the altar. To avoid trouble he made himself scarce when the rituals began.

His parents knew now that one day he would take a Muslim name. That upset them a great deal. They were Taoist-Buddhists, and as a bomoh Rashid's father had a position in the community. Rashid was as conciliatory as he could be; he didn't argue. He never wanted to hurt their feelings.

All this was in 1973. Rashid was in his eighteenth year.

It occurred to me, hearing his story, that four years before, in 1969, there had been terrible racial riots in Malaysia between Chinese and Malays. I asked Rashid about that time.

He said, "All of us were affected. I was in form two. The riots started on May the thirteenth. I was thirteen plus. Thirteen years, six months. I remember cycling to school and finding the place deserted, the streets deserted. And then we saw some people coming back this way, and they all called out to me, 'Go back! Go back!' This was very early in the morning. By eight or nine everybody knew what was going on."

The family had to survive for some months on what they had at home. Rice, salted fish, salted black beans. They had no fresh food. Rashid's father had no savings. Because of the curfew people couldn't come to him. So he had no income, no tribute. It was a time of great hardship for the family. After a few weeks the curfew was lifted, but the fear was so great that for three months people didn't leave their houses. There were stories of

Malays rounding up Chinese people, loading them onto trucks, executing them, and then dumping the bodies. There were stories, too, of Malays being hacked to death by Chinese gangsters.

Gradually things calmed down. Classes started up again at the schools. The bomoh, born on an Indonesian island in the last century to a Chinese father and a Malay mother, would have always known about Malay hate, Malay racial rage. Yet, perhaps because of his work, which brought sufferers and suppliants of all sorts to him, he felt that people were people. He refused to believe that human beings could cease being human, and he told his children so. He refused to believe the stories that were brought to him of Malay soldiers going round the country shooting Chinese people. He was never vengeful or bitter.

But it could not have been easy for him when, four years after that terror, his son became a Muslim and took the name of Rashid and stayed away from the old rituals of the house. He hadn't minded when his two sons sang hymns about Jesus in the temple. But becoming a Muslim was something else. It would have seemed like a turning away from the family. The bomoh could be philosophical about the riots; but the antagonism between Malay and Chinese went deep; it couldn't be wished away. Officially in Malaysia to be a Malay was to be Muslim.

And, though Rashid didn't say so, it was the race riots

of 1969 that had given a push to the Malay movement and the new Islam among the young.

There were twenty people in the house, and Rashid (when he got to the higher forms of the secondary school) could begin to study only at about midnight, when the television was turned off and people went to sleep. He would sit on his father's bomoh chair in the living room, the chair on which his father sat when, sometimes in a trance, he received people and gave his consultations, and he would study or read or write for three or four hours. That was where, below the deities of snow and fire and sword, he read Shakespeare and Jane Austen and Dickens, and wrote his essays, and studied for his examinations. He never thought he was suffering hardship; that idea came to him much later, when life was easier.

His time in the family house came to an end when he finished at the secondary school and went on to the university in Kuala Lumpur. He did English. It was an insubstantial thing to do, but—from the account he gave—he was going to the university really to be free. He was able to support himself. The tuition fees were low. And he was able to earn enough in the long vacation doing various jobs to pay for his lodging in the college. He taught; he did little jobs in the media and advertising.

He didn't take his studies seriously. He spent so little

time at lectures that in his second year the university authorities gave him an ultimatum. A fatherly Indian tutor helped him to pull himself together, and in the end he was able to get a reasonable second-class degree. In the three years he spent at the university he went home only once, for a week. That was in his second year. After he got his degree, at the end of his third year, he began to work full-time in Kuala Lumpur; and he couldn't even think of going home.

The insubstantial English degree didn't help him get a job, and he began to do full-time what he had done in the vacations. What had been exciting in the beginning, part of his freedom, soon became tedious. He could make a living, but his life was unfocused and disordered. Without Islam—which mattered more and more, and had mattered even at the university—his life would have been without point.

He was driving to work one day when a traffic policeman signaled to him to stop. He rolled down the window and said, "What's wrong?" There was something in Rashid's manner that enraged the policeman. He said to Rashid, "What do you mean, 'What's wrong?' It's 'What's wrong, *sir*?'" And he began to write out a ticket.

The policeman was Indian. It was well known in Kuala Lumpur—so Rashid said—that Indians became arrogant in power. And, though Rashid didn't say, the Indian policeman might have been especially rough with Rashid because he was a Chinese. Rashid said in his heart, I will fix you up. I will get even. You just wait.

Rashid decided at that moment that he was going to join the police, to "invest in power." The decision was sudden, but he had been thinking about it for some time. For some time he had been dreaming of wearing a police uniform, to win respect from people, and to protect himself from people like the Indian policeman and from security guards who chased him away from parking spaces reserved for dignitaries.

What came out now was that Rashid's eldest brother was high in the police. This brother was a full twenty years older than Rashid, and Rashid would not have seen much of him. He had joined the police force as a constable and—he was another son with the bomoh's energy and drive—he had risen through the ranks, becoming first an inspector, and then a gazetted officer. Rashid had a childhood memory of this brother coming to the family house in his inspector's uniform. At some point the local police station needed to contact the inspector—no telephone in the bomoh's house at that time—and a police sergeant came to the house and saluted the inspector in front of the whole family. This excited the children. Rashid also remembered the inspector's handgun.

Rashid said, "The whole idea of putting on this uniform with the three pips on the shoulder gets the adrenaline pumping. On reflection it all seems silly, but it was real then. Once you had the power"—and Rashid was telling the story from his later position of ease and security and influence—"it was very different altogether."

Rashid also felt that, after his too-liberated time at the university, and his unfocused freelance career afterwards, he needed order and discipline, even regimentation, in his life again. He thought the police force would do that for him. And though his insecurity and aggressiveness and drive to power (as he thought) were real enough at the time, he recognized with a part of his mind that his approach was contrary to his upbringing.

He said, "My father and my brother had different kinds of power. My brother had authority. My father had the respect due to his gifts, and also because he was a very generous man. Which was why, when the riots came, we had a very tough time. We had no savings. My father would buy four or five loaves of bread from the bread man because he didn't have the heart to tell him no—it didn't matter how much bread we had. And I still do that today when the bread man comes. And the policy was to give more than the price of the bread. He never took change. He said, 'With these people you must not be calculating.'"

It was a year before Rashid could join the police. Five hundred applications were processed; many more had been received. After physical and classroom tests two hundred and fifty were called in for the first induction. One hundred got through the formal interviews; that took some months. Examinations and intelligence tests then sifted out half of those. At the end twenty were chosen and sent to the police training school; Rashid was one of them.

He gave himself a new haircut for the training school. The first thing he and the others had to do was to get their heads shaved by the training school barber. He had joined the police for the sake of power. His first experience as a trainee officer was this ritual humiliation.

And for the next two months he and the others were at the mercy of sergeants and constables. The police training rules hadn't changed since the British time. Small misdemeanors—like talking on parade—could be severely punished, with an hour's double-time marching in full uniform in the heat, with an M-16 rifle held in a position that after a while caused fine, excruciating pain in the triceps and elbow.

At the end of his two months he had, indeed, become disciplined. The urge to power, the constant little urges to get even when the time came with the sergeants and constables who were roughing him up, had been burnt away. He even felt regard for the men who had trained him.

When he had graduated and been commissioned he went to see his father. He hadn't seen him for some years. Rashid knew now that the bomoh would be proud of him; and the bomoh was very proud of him.

Rashid said, "He was very happy to receive me. In his eyes his son had been transformed. My Muslim conversion wasn't brought up any more. I had sent him a photograph of me in uniform, with my name tag, with my Muslim name, RASHID. And he had it hanging on the wall of the living room."

To be a police officer was to do more than wear the uniform and receive salutes. It was constantly to see, in the rough area where he had been posted, dead men, mutilated corpses, cruelty. Rashid soon couldn't take any more. He joined the intelligence service. It had not figured in his fantasy of power; but he understood now that in the police that was where the real power lay. But he didn't like it. He had lost his taste for police work.

He thought of the law. He had been told by one of his police instructors, while he was training, that he reasoned like a good lawyer. That had stayed with him; and after less than four years in the police he resigned, did a business job for a while for the money, and enrolled in the law course at the university. It was what he was born for; the law engaged all his instincts; he was successful from the start. The Malaysian boom had made it possible for him to chop and change as he had done; in an earlier time he would have had to be more cautious, to stay with what he had found.

He said, "Though now I am in touch with sources of power, all that excitement that consumed me in those days is not there now. Looking back, I feel that all the stages I had to go through were necessary. The stages of my childhood, the conditions I was brought up in, the opportunities, helped me to be self-sustaining."

His background had made him a very positive sort of person. He didn't moan and groan. He didn't think that was because he was Chinese; he had Chinese friends who moaned and groaned. He thought it was something he got from his father. He never knew his father to complain. He suffered much pain from a hernia, but he told no one about it. He had a problem with his spine that kept him in constant pain.

Rashid went to see him a few months before he died. He was eighty-eight, and was bedridden. His body had wasted away. He had lost about thirty or forty pounds. He had shrunk.

Rashid said, "Father, you have grown so thin."

The bomoh said, "Everything is O.K. I am fine." But there were tears in his eyes.

Rashid, seeing his father so close to death, thought of his hard childhood, and of all that he had managed to do. All his children, so many of them born at an unpromising time, were now well placed.

Rashid said, "When I was having fantasies of power, even before I was a policeman, he was exercising real power." As a bomoh. "Compared to him, I was, year to year, infantile. I will not tolerate any kind of criticism of him, not even from members of the family. What he did we saw with our own eyes. He did not have to make a proclamation of his power. It may be that I have a direct affinity with my father. He was an eighth son. I was an eighth son. I was told by my mother that I look exactly like my father. My mother is not very good with words. She doesn't go around flattering people."

Rashid's father didn't want anyone to follow his calling as a bomoh, or to profess his faith. He just wanted his children to go through the rituals. Rashid couldn't do that when he became a Muslim. But it pleased Rashid that his mother did the rituals, and that when she died, other members of the family would be carrying on her worship of her Malay datuk spirit in her kitchen, and doing the rituals on the family altar.

from HALF A LIFE

Roger said one day, "My editor is coming to London soon. You know I do him a weekly letter about books and plays. I also drop the odd word about cultural personalities. He pays me ten pounds a week. I suppose he's coming to check on me. He says he wants to meet my friends. I've promised him an intellectual London dinner party, and you must come, Willie. It will be the first party in the Marble Arch house. I'll present you as a literary star to be. In Proust there's a social figure called Swann. He likes sometimes for his own pleasure to bring together dissimilar people, to create a social nosegay, as he says. I am hoping to do something like that for the editor. There'll be a Negro I met in West Africa when I did my National Service. He is the son of a West Indian who went to live in West Africa as part of the Back to Africa movement. His name is Marcus, after the black crook who founded the movement. You'll like him. He's very charming, very urbane. He is dedicated to interracial sex and is quite insatiable. When we first met in West Africa his talk was almost all about sex. To keep my end up I said that African women were attractive. He said, 'If you like the animal thing.' He is now training to be a diplomat for when his country becomes independent, and to him London is paradise. He has two ambitions. The first is to have a grandchild who will be pure white in appearance. He is halfway there. He has five mulatto children, by five white women, and he feels that all he has to do now is to keep an eye on the children and make sure they don't let him down. He wants when he is old to walk down the King's Road with this white grandchild. People will stare and the child will say, loudly, 'What are they staring at, Grandfather?' His second ambition is to be the first black man to have an account at Coutts. That's the Queen's bank."

Willie said, "Don't they have black people?"

"I don't know. I don't think he really knows either."

"Why doesn't he just go to the bank and find out? Ask for a form."

"He feels they might put him off in a discreet way. They might say they've run out of forms. He doesn't want that to happen. He will go to Coutts and ask to open an account only when he is sure that they'll take him. He wants to do it very casually, and he must be the first black man to do it. It's all very involved and I can't say I understand it. But you'll talk to him about it. He's quite open. It's part of his charm. There will also be a young poet and his wife. You should have no trouble with them. They will look disapproving and say absolutely nothing, and the poet will be waiting to snub anyone who talks to him. So you don't have to say anything to him. He is actually quite well known. My editor will be very pleased to meet him. In a foolish moment I wrote a friendly paragraph about one of the poet's books in a London Letter, and word somehow got back to him. That's how I've been landed with him."

Willie said, "I know about silent people. My father was always on a vow of silence. I'll look the poet up."

"It won't give you any pleasure. The poetry is complicated and showing off and perfectly arid, and you can think for some time that it's your fault it's like that. That's how I was taken in. Look him up if you want, but you mustn't feel you have to do it before the dinner. I'm asking the poet and his wife only for the nosegay effect. A little bit of dead fern, to set the whole thing off. The people you should study are two men I've known since Oxford. They are both of modest middle-class backgrounds and they pursue rich women. They do other things, but this is actually their career. Very rich women. It began in a small way at Oxford, and since then they have moved up and up, higher and higher, to richer and richer women. Their standards of wealth in a woman are now very high indeed. They are bitter enemies, of course. Each thinks the other is a fraud. It's been an education to see them operate. They both at about the same time in Oxford made the discovery that in the pursuit of rich women the first conquest is all-important. It piques the interest of other rich women, who might otherwise pay no attention to a middle-class adventurer, and it brings these women into the hunter's orbit. Soon the competition is among the rich women, each claiming to be richer than the other.

"Richard is ill-favored and drunken and loud, and getting fat, not the kind of man you would think women would be attracted to. He wears grubby tweed jackets and dirty Viyella shirts. But he knows his market, and some of that coarseness is an act and is part of his bait. He presents himself as a kind of Bertolt Brecht, the promiscuous and smelly German communist playwright. But Richard is only a bedroom Marxist. Marxism takes him to the bedroom, and Marxism stops in the bedroom. All the women he seduces know that. They feel safe with him. It was like that in Oxford and it's still like that. The difference is that at Oxford it thrilled his common soul just to sleep with rich women, and now he takes large sums of money off them. Of course he's made his mistakes. I imagine there has been more than one bedroom confrontation. I imag-

ine a half-dressed lady saying tearfully, 'I thought you
were a Marxist.' I imagine Richard pulling on his trousers
fast and saying, 'thought you were rich.' Richard is in
publishing, quite rich now, and rising fast. As a publisher
his Marxism makes him more attractive than ever. The
more he takes off the ladies the more other ladies rush to
give him.

"Peter's style is entirely different. His background is
more modest, country estate agent, and at Oxford he
began to develop his English-gentleman style. Oxford is
full of young foreign women studying English at various
language schools. Some of them are rich. Peter by some
instinct ignored the university women and chose to operate among these people. They would have thought him
the genuine article, and he, quicker than they, learning
soon to sort the wheat from the chaff, scored some
notable successes. He was invited to two or three rich
European houses. He began to meet rich people on the
Continent. He cultivated his appearance. He began to
wear his hair in a kind of semi-military style, rising flat
above the ears, and he learned to work his lantern jaws.
One day in the junior common room, when we were
having bad coffee after lunch, he said to me, 'What would
you say is the sexiest thing a man can wear?' I was taken
aback. This wasn't typical common-room conversation.
But it showed how far Peter had got from estate-agenting,
and where he was going. He said at last, 'A very clean and

well-ironed white shirt.' A French girl he'd slept with the night before had told him that. And he's worn nothing but white shirts ever since. They are very expensive now, handmade, very fine two-ply or three-ply cotton, the collar fitting close to his neck and riding well above the jacket at the back. He likes them starched in a certain way, so that the collar looks waxed. He is an academic, an historian. He's written a little book about food in history—an important subject, but a scrappy little anthology of a book—and he talks about new books and big advances from publishers, but that's only for show. His intellectual energy has actually become very low. The women consume him. To satisfy them he has developed what I can only describe as a special sexual taste. Women talk—never forget that, Willie—and word of this taste of Peter's has spread. It is now part of his success. His academic interests have always reflected the women he's been involved with. He's become a Latin-American expert, and now he's got a great prize. A Colombian woman. Colombia is a poor country, but she's connected to one of those absurd Latin-American fortunes that have been created out of four centuries of Indian blood and bones. She's coming with Peter, and Richard will be tormented by the most exquisite jealousy. He won't take it quietly. He will do something, create some fierce Marxist scene. I'll arrange it so that you talk to the lady. That's our nosegay. Our little dinner party for ten."

Willie went away counting. He could only count nine. He wondered who the tenth person was.

On another day Roger said, "My editor wants to stay with me. I've told him the house is very small, but he says he grew up in poverty and knows about back-to-back houses. The house really has only a bedroom and a half. The editor is a very big man, and I suppose I will have to take the half bedroom. Or go to a hotel. That'll be unusual. I'll be like a guest at my own dinner party."

On the day Willie knocked and waited for some time at the door of the little house. At last Perdita let him in. Willie didn't recognize her right away. The editor was already there. He was very fat, with glasses, bursting out of his shirt, and Willie felt it was his shyness, an unwillingness to be seen, that had made him not want to stay at a hotel. He seemed to take up a lot of room in the house, which in spite of all the little tricks of the architect was really very small. Roger, oppressed-looking, came up from the basement and did the introductions.

The editor remained sitting down. He said he saw Mahatma Gandhi in 1931 when the mahatma came to England for the Round Table Conference. He said nothing else about the mahatma (whom Willie and his mother and his mother's uncle despised), nothing about the mahatma's clothes or appearance; he spoke only of seeing him. When Marcus, the West Indian West African, came, the editor told in a similar way about seeing Paul Robeson.

Marcus looked confident and humorous and full of zest, and as soon as he began to talk Willie was captivated. Willie said, "I've been hearing about your plans for a white grandchild." Marcus said, "It's not so extraordinary. It'll only be repeating something that happened on a large scale here a hundred and fifty years ago. In the eighteenth century there were about half a million black people in England. They've all vanished. They've disappeared in the local population. They were bred out. The Negro gene is a recessive one. If this were more widely known there would be a good deal less racial feeling than there is. And a lot of that feeling is only skin deep, so to speak. I'll tell you this story. When I was in Africa I got to know a Frenchwoman from Alsace. She said after a time that she wanted me to meet her family. We went to Europe together and went to her hometown. She introduced me to her school friends. They were conservative people and she was worried about what they would think. In the fortnight I was there I screwed them all. I even screwed two or three of the mothers. But my friend was still worried."

The poet, when he came, received his homage from the editor, and then he and his wife sat sullenly together in one corner of the little room.

The Colombian woman was older than Willie expected. She might have been in her late forties. Her name was Serafina. She was slender, delicate, worried-looking. Her hair was black enough to suggest a dye, and her skin was very white and powdered up to the hair. When eventually she came and sat next to Willie she said, "Do you like ladies?" When Willie hesitated she said, "Not all men like ladies. I know. I was a virgin until I was twenty-six. My husband was a pederast. Colombia is full of little mestizo boys you can buy for a dollar." Willie said, "What happened when you were twenty-six?" She said, "I am telling you my life story, but I am not in the confessional. Obviously something happened." When Perdita and Roger began to pass the food around she said, "I love men. I think they have a cosmic strength." Willie said, "You mean energy?" She said with irritation, "I mean cosmic strength." Willie looked at Peter. He had prepared for the evening. He was wearing his expensive-looking white shirt with the starched, waxy collar high at the back; his semi-military blond-and-gray hair was flat at the sides, with just a touch of pomade to keep it in order; but his eyes were dim and fatigued and far away.

Roger, passing with food, said, "Why did you marry a pederast, Serafina?" She said, "We are rich and white." Roger said, "That's hardly a reason." She ignored that. She said, "We have been rich and white for generations. We speak classical Spanish. My father was this white and handsome man. You should have seen him. It is hard for us to get married in Colombia." Willie said, "Aren't there other white people in Colombia?" Serafina said, "It is a common word for you here. It isn't for us. We are rich and white in Colombia and we speak this pure old Spanish, purer than the Spanish they speak in Spain. It is hard for us to get husbands. Many of our girls have married Europeans. My younger sister is married to an Argentine. When you have to look so hard and so far for a husband you can make mistakes."

Richard the publisher called out from across the room, "I would say it's a mistake. Leaving Colombia and going to live on stolen Indian land."

Serafina said, "My sister has stolen no land."

Richard said, "It was stolen for her eighty years ago. By General Roca and his gang. The railway and the Remington rifle against Indian slings and stones. That's how the pampas were won, and all those bogus smart estancias. So your sister moved from old plunder to new theft. Thank God for Eva Perón, I say. Pulling down the whole rotten edifice."

Serafina said to Willie, "This man is trying to make himself interesting to me. It's a common type in Colombia."

Marcus said, "I don't think many people know that there were large Negro populations in Buenos Aires and Uruguay in 1800. They disappeared in the local population. They were bred out. The Negro gene is recessive. Not many people know that."

Richard and Marcus carried on the cross-room talk, Richard always moving around what Marcus said and aiming to be provocative. Serafina said to Willie, "He is the kind of man who will try to seduce me as soon as he is alone with me. It is boring. He thinks I am Latin American and easy." She went silent. Through all of this Peter remained perfectly calm. Willie, no longer having to listen, and idly looking around the room, let his eyes rest on Perdita and her long upper body. He did not think her beautiful, but he remembered the elegant way she slapped the striped gloves down on the Chez Victor table, and at the same time he thought of June undressing in the room in Notting Hill. Perdita caught his gaze and held it. Willie was inexpressibly stirred.

Roger and Perdita began clearing away the plates. Marcus, in his brisk, zestful way, got up and began to help. Coffee and brandy came.

Serafina said absently to Willie, "Have you felt jealousy?" Her thoughts had been running along ways he didn't know. Willie said, "Not yet. I have only felt desire." She said, "Listen to this. When I took Peter to Colombia the women all ran to him. This English gentleman and scholar with the strong jawline. After one month he forgot everything I had done for him and he ran away with somebody else. But he didn't know the country, and he made a big mistake. The woman had fooled him. She was a mestiza and she wasn't rich at all. He found out in a week. He came back to me and begged to be forgiven. He knelt on the floor and put his head in my lap and cried like a child. I stroked his hair and said, 'You thought she was rich? You thought she was white?' He said, 'Yes, yes.' I forgave him. But perhaps he should be punished. What do you think?"

The editor cleared his throat once, twice. It was his call for silence. Serafina, turning away from Willie, and looking away from Richard, sat up straight and fixed her gaze on the editor. He sat big and heavy in his corner, overflowing the waistband of his trousers, his shirt pulling at every button.

He said, "I don't think any of you here can understand what an occasion this evening has been for a provincial editor. You have each one of you given me a glimpse of a world far removed from my own. I come from a smoky old town in the dark satanic north. Not many people want to know about us nowadays. But we have played our part in history. Our factories made goods that went all over the world, and wherever our goods went they helped to usher in the modern age. We quite rightly thought of ourselves as the center of the world. But now the world has tilted, and it is only when I meet people like yourselves that I get some idea where the world is going. So this occasion is full of ironies. You have all led glittering lives. I have heard of some of you by report, and everything I have seen and heard here tonight has confirmed what I have heard. I wish from the bottom of my heart to thank you all for the great courtesy you have shown a man whose life has been the opposite of glittering. But we who live in dark corners have our souls. We have had our ambitions, we have had our dreams, and life can play cruel tricks on us. 'Perhaps in this neglected spot is laid some heart once pregnant with celestial fire.' I cannot hope to match the poet Gray, but I have written in my own way of a heart like that. And I would like now, with your permission, and before we separate, perhaps forever, to make you an offering of what I have written."

From the inner breast pocket of his jacket the editor took out some folded sheets of newsprint. Deliberately, in the silence he had created, looking at no one, he shook out the sheets.

He said, "These are galleys, newspaper proofs. The copy itself has been long prepared. A word or two may be changed here and there, an awkward phrase or two put right, but by and large it is ready for the press. It will be printed in my paper in the week of my death. You will guess that it is my obituary. Some of you may gasp. Some of you may sigh. But death comes to all, and it is better to be prepared. These words were composed in no spirit of vainglory. You know me well enough to know that. And it is, rather, in a spirit of sorrow, and regret for all the might-have-beens, that I invite you now to contemplate the course of an obscure provincial life."

He began to read. *"Henry Arthur Percival Somers, who became editor of this paper in the dark days of November 1940,*

*and whose death is reported more fully on another page, was born
the son of a ship's fitter on 17 July 1895. . . ."*

Stage by stage, galley by galley, one narrow column of
print to a galley, the story unfolded: the little house, the
poor street, the father's periods of unemployment, family
bereavements, the boy leaving school at fourteen, doing
little clerking jobs in various offices, the war, his rejection
by the army on medical grounds; and then at last, in the last
year of the war, his job on the newspaper, on the production side, as a "copy-holder," really a woman's job, reading
copy aloud to the typesetter. As he read his emotion grew.

The poet and his wife looked on aloof and unsurprised
and disdaining. Peter was vacant. Serafina held herself
upright and showed her profile to Richard. Marcus, men-
tally restless, thinking of this and that, more than once
began to talk about something quite unrelated, and then
stopped at the sound of his own voice. But Willie was fascinated by the editor's story. To him it was all new. There
were not many concrete details to hold on to, but he was
trying as he listened to see the editor's town and to enter
the editor's life. He found himself, to his surprise, thinking of his own father; and then he began to think about
himself. Sitting beside Serafina, who had turned away
from him, and was stiff, resisting conversation, Willie
leaned forward to concentrate on the editor.

He, the editor, was aware of Willie's interest, and he

weakened. He began to choke on his words. Once or twice he sobbed. And then he was on the last galley. Tears were running down his face. He seemed about to break down. *". . . His deepest life was in the mind. But journalism is by its nature ephemeral, and he left no memorial. Love, the divine illusion, never touched him. But he had a lifelong romance with the English language."* He took off his misted glasses, held the galleys in his left hand, and fixed his wet eyes on a spot on the floor three or four feet in front of him. There was a great silence.

Marcus said, "That was a very nice piece of writing."

The editor remained as he had been, looking down at the floor, letting the tears flow, and silence came back to the room. The party was over. When people spoke, saying good-bye, it was in whispers, as in a sickroom. The poet and his wife left; it was as though they hadn't been. Serafina stood up, let her gaze sweep unseeing past Richard, and took Peter away. Marcus whispered, "Let me help you clear away, Perdita." Willie was surprised by a pang of jealousy. But neither he nor Marcus was allowed to stay.

Roger, saying good-bye to them at the door of the little house, lost his worried look. He said mischievously, not raising his voice, "He told me he wanted to meet my London friends. I had no idea he wanted an audience."

Among the Believers
On the basis of his seven-month journey across the Asian continent, V. S. Naipaul explores the life, the culture, and the ongoing ferment inside four nations of Islam: Iran, Pakistan, Malaysia, and Indonesia. In this brilliant account, Naipaul depicts an Islamic world at odds with the contemporary world and fueled by an implacable determination to believe.
Current Affairs/0-394-71195-5

An Area of Darkness
A classic of modern travel writing, *An Area of Darkness* is V. S. Naipaul's profound reckoning with his ancestral homeland and an extraordinarily perceptive chronicle of his first encounter with India. Traveling from the bureaucratic morass of Bombay to the ethereal beauty of Kashmir and a sacred ice cave in the Himalayas, Naipaul encounters a dizzying cross section of humanity and develops strikingly original and passionate responses to the subcontinent.
Travel/0-375-70835-9

A Bend in the River
In this novel V. S. Naipaul takes us deeply into the life of one man—an Indian who, uprooted by the bloody tides of Third World history, has come to live in an isolated town at the bend of a great river in a newly independent

African nation. Naipaul gives us the most convincing and disturbing vision yet of what happens in a place caught between the dangerously alluring modern world and its own tenacious past and traditions.

Fiction/Literature/0-679-72202-5

Between Father and Son

In 1950, V. S. Naipaul, aged seventeen, took a two-week journey by steamer and arrived in Oxford, England, a world utterly removed from the one he had longed to escape and to which he would never really return. This collection of letters between a sacrificing father and his determined son gives us an intimate view of Naipaul's formative years and bears witness to the flowering of a literary genius.

Biography/0-375-70726-3

Beyond Belief

Fourteen years after the publication of his landmark travel narrative *Among the Believers,* V. S. Naipaul returned to the four non-Arab Islamic countries he reported on so vividly at the time of Ayatollah Khomeini's triumph in Iran. *Beyond Belief* is the result of his five-month journey through Indonesia, Iran, Pakistan, and Malaysia. In extended conversations with a vast number of people, including a rare survivor of the martyr brigades of the Iran-Iraq war and an intellectual training as a Marxist guerrilla, Naipaul deliberately effaces himself to let the voices of his subjects come through.

Current Affairs/0-375-70648-8

The Enigma of Arrival

The story of a writer's singular journey—from one place to another, from the British colony of Trinidad to the ancient countryside of England and from one state of mind to another—this is perhaps V. S. Naipaul's most autobiographical work. Yet it is also woven through with remarkable invention to make it a rich and complex novel.
Fiction/Literature/0-394-75760-2

Guerrillas

On a troubled Caribbean island—where Asians, Africans, Americans, and former British colonials coexist in a state of suppressed hysteria—a white man arrives with his mistress, an Englishwoman inflamed by fantasies of native power and sexuality, unaware of the consequences of her actions. Together with a young mulatto leader of the "Revolution," they act out a gripping drama of death, sexual violence, and political and spiritual impotence that illuminates the ravages of history on individual lives.
Fiction/Literature/0-679-73174-1

Half a Life

Half a Life is the story of Willie Chandran, whose father turned his back on his brahmin heritage and married a woman of low caste—a disastrous union he would live to regret. As an adult, Willie's flight from the travails of his mixed birth takes him to London, where, in the shabby haunts of immigrants and literary bohemians of the 1950s, he tries to contrive a new identity. His struggle to defeat self-doubt and become a writer bring him to the brink of exhaustion, from which he is rescued only by the love of a good woman.

Fiction/Literature/0-375-70728-X

A House for Mr. Biswas

All his life, Mr. Mohun Biswas has been trying to achieve some semblance of independence, only to face a lifetime of calamity. Shuttled from one residence to another after the drowning of his father, Mr. Biswas yearns for a place he can call home. But when he marries into the domineering Tulsi family on whom he indignantly becomes dependent, Mr. Biswas embarks on an arduous and endless effort to weaken their hold over him and purchase a house of his own.

Fiction/Literature/0-375-70716-6

In a Free State

It begins as a simple car trip through Africa. Two English people—Bobby, a civil servant with a guilty appetite for African boys, and Linda, a supercilious "compound wife"—are driving back to their enclave after a stay in the capital. But in between lies the landscape of an unnamed country whose squalor and ethnic bloodletting suggest Idi Amin's Uganda. And the farther V. S. Naipaul's protagonists travel into it, the more they find themselves crossing the line that separates privileged outsiders from horrified victims.

Fiction/Literature/1-4000-3055-2

India: A Wounded Civilization

In 1975, at the height of Indira Gandhi's "Emergency," V. S. Naipaul returned to India, the country his ancestors had left one hundred years earlier. Drawing on novels, news reports, political memoirs, and his own encounters with ordinary Indians—from a supercilious prince to an engineer constructing housing for Bombay's homeless—Naipaul captures a vast, mysterious, and agonized continent inaccessible to foreigners and barely visible to its own people.

History/Travel/1-4000-3075-7

The Loss of El Dorado

The history of Trinidad begins with a delusion: the belief that somewhere nearby on the South American mainland lay El Dorado, the mythical kingdom of gold. In this extraordinary and often gripping book, V. S. Naipaul—himself a native of Trinidad—shows how that delusion drew a small island into the vortex of world events, making it the object of Spanish and English colonial designs and a mecca for treasure-seekers, slave-traders, and revolutionaries.

History/1-4000-3076-5

The Middle Passage

In this masterpiece of travel writing first published in 1962, V. S. Naipaul returned to Trinidad, his country of origin, and also visited British Guiana (now Guyana), Surinam, Martinique, and Jamaica. Interpreting their present characters in light of their past histories as British,

Dutch, and French territories built on slave labor, Naipaul relates the ghastly episodes of the region's colonial past and shows how they continue to inform its language, politics, and values.

History/0-375-70834-0

Miguel Street

Miguel Street is a derelict corner of Trinidad's capital that is full of unique characters. There's Popo the carpenter, who attempts to build "the thing without a name"; the mad Man-man, who goes from running for public office to staging his own crucifixion; and the dreaded Big Foot, the bully with glass tear ducts. Then there's the lovely Mrs. Hereira, in thrall to her monstrous husband. Set during World War II and narrated by an unnamed but precociously observant neighborhood boy, *Miguel Street* overflows with life on every page.

Fiction/Literature/0-375-71387-5

The Mimic Men

Born of Indian heritage and raised on a British–dependent Caribbean island, Ralph Singh has retired to London, writing his memoirs to impose order on his chaotic existence. As he assesses his childhood and his short-lived marriage to an ostentatious white woman, Singh realizes what has kept him from becoming a proper Englishman. A profound novel of cultural displacement, *The Mimic Men* artfully evokes a colonial man's experience in a post-colonial world.

Fiction/Literature/0-375-70717-4

The Mystic Masseur

In 1940s Trinidad, masseurs were the medical practitioners of choice. Ganesh Ramsumair, a failed schoolteacher and impecunious village masseur, in time becomes a revered mystic, a thriving entrepreneur, and a beloved politician. Ganesh's ascent is both aided and impeded by his wife, his father-in-law, and his patients. Witty and tender, *The Mystic Masseur* is V. S. Naipaul at his most expansive and evocative.

Fiction/Literature/0-375-70714-X

The Nightwatchman's Occurrence Book

V. S. Naipaul's legendary command of broad comedy and acute social observation is on abundant display in these classic works of fiction—two novels and a collection of stories—that capture the rhythms of life in the Caribbean and England with impressive subtlety and humor. *The Suffrage of Elvira, Mr. Stone and the Knights Companion,* and *A Flag on the Island* are unfailingly stylish, filled with intelligence and feeling.

Fiction/Literature/0-375-70833-2

A Turn in the South

In the tradition of political and cultural revelation that V. S. Naipaul has so brilliantly made his own, *A Turn in the South,* his first book about the United States, is a revealing, disturbing, elegiac book about the American South—from Atlanta to Charleston, Tallahassee to Tuskegee, Nashville to Chapel Hill.

Nonfiction/Literature/0-679-72488-5

A Way in the World

Spanning continents and centuries, *A Way in the World* tells intersecting stories whose protagonists include the half-demented Sir Walter Raleigh fruitlessly seeking El Dorado in the New World; the nineteenth-century insurgent Francisco Miranda, who in his quest to liberate South America becomes entangled in his own fantasies and borrowed ideas; and the doomed Blair, a present-day Caribbean revolutionary stranded—and eventually martyred—in East Africa.

Fiction/Literature/0-679-76166-7

The Writer and the World

Spanning four decades and four continents, this magisterial volume brings together the essential shorter works of reflection and reportage by our most sensitive, literate, and undeceivable observer of the post-colonial world. In its pages V. S. Naipaul trains his relentless moral intelligence on societies from India to the United States and sees how each deals with the challenges of modernity and the seductions of both the real and mythical past.

Literary Criticism/0-375-70730-1

VINTAGE **READERS**

Authors available in this series

Martin Amis

James Baldwin

Sandra Cisneros

Joan Didion

Richard Ford

Langston Hughes

Barry Lopez

Alice Munro

Haruki Murakami

Vladimir Nabokov

V. S. Naipaul

Oliver Sacks

Representing a wide spectrum of some of our most significant modern authors, the Vintage Readers offer an attractive, accessible selection of writing that matters.